# FOUR LAKES RANCH

*A Montana Country Inn Romance Novel - Book 5*

## AMY RAFFERTY

## STAY UPDATED WITH ME

Thank you so much for purchasing or downloading my book! I am grateful to all my amazing readers.

To stay updated on all my latest books, newsletters, freebies and beautiful photos from the fabulous locations I write about, why not join my VIP group?

I will send you regular pictures of La Jolla Cove, San Diego and the Florida Gulf Beaches where I try to spend as much time as I can. I live in San Diego, my own 'Garden Of Eden' and I am in love with the sea and the beaches in the area. They inspire me to write lots of beachy mystery romance fiction to share with my awesome readers like you. To join me go to https://landing.mailer lite.com/webforms/landing/y6w2d2

You will be asked for your email. You also get a FREE BOOK whenever you sign-up!

# FREE BOOK

To get your FREE copy of Cody Bay Inn Prequel - Nantucket Calling go to www.amazon.com/B0992NFTY1

# CHARACTER LIST

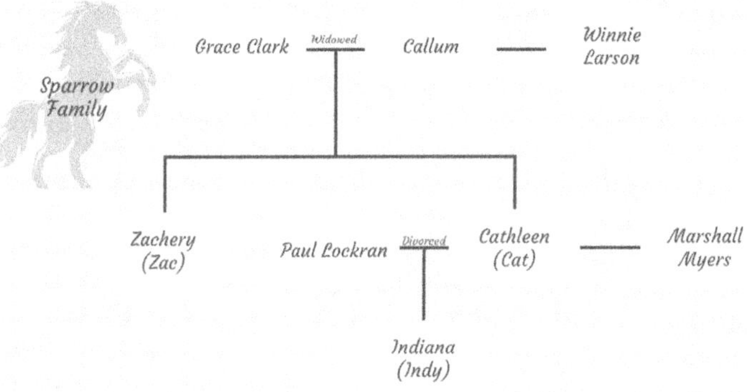


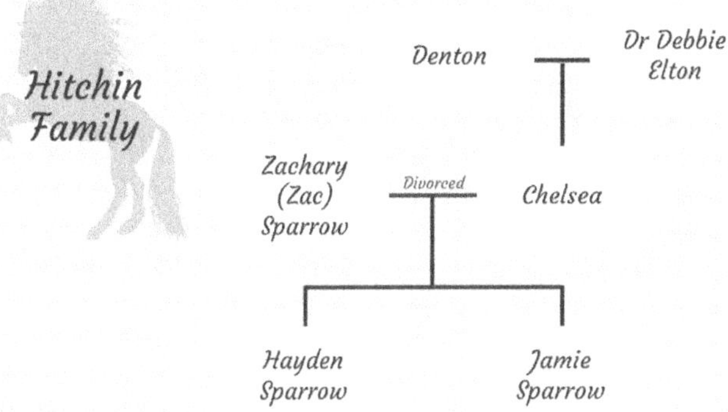

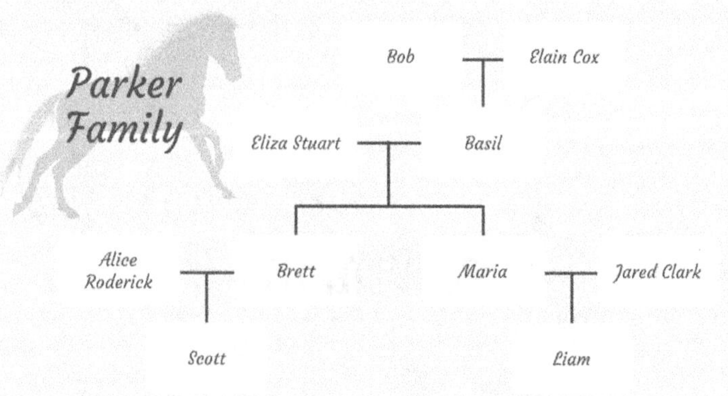

Parker Family
Bob
Elain Cox
Eliza Stuart
Basil
Alice Roderick
Brett
Maria
Jared Clark
Scott
Liam


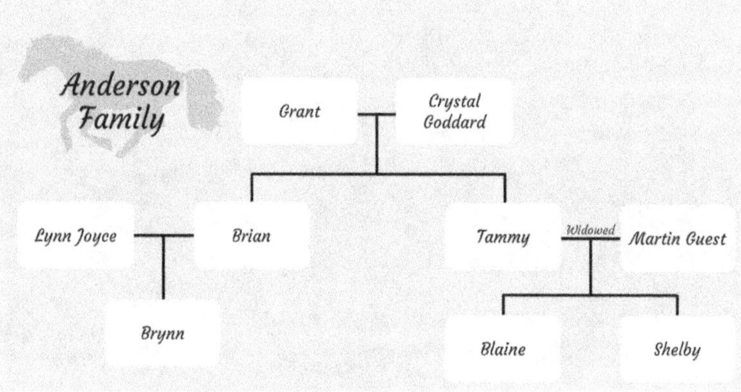

Anderson Family
Grant
Crystal Goddard
Lynn Joyce
Brian
Tammy
Widowed
Martin Guest
Brynn
Blaine
Shelby


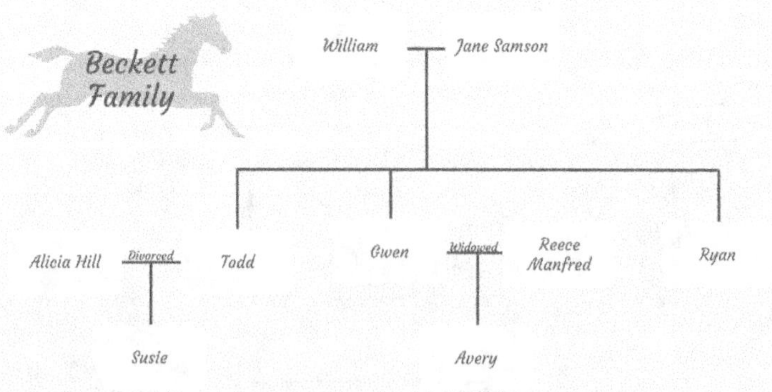

Beckett Family
William
Jane Samson
Alicia Hill
Divorced
Todd
Gwen
Widowed
Reece Manfred
Ryan
Susie
Avery

# MAP OF THE RANCHES

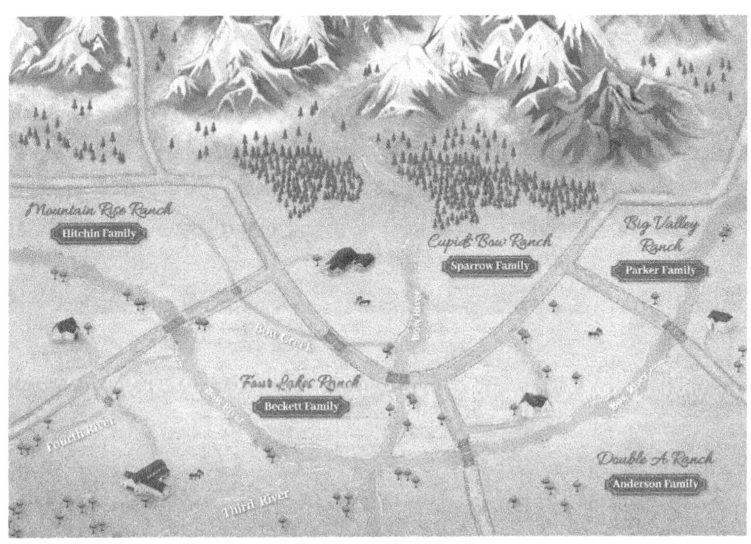

# Chapter One

# WELCOME TO THE GROUP, TAMMY

Tammy knew she was being a coward, but she'd rather avoid any weird awkwardness. She was waiting for everyone to get up before slipping down to breakfast. The girls were still on a school break and were only due back next week, so there was no need for her to be the first one awake. Tammy kept her ears open, waiting to hear Brynn stir and bolt out of her room with three bassets trailing her. Even if Tammy was still asleep, that would wake her up. At least if there was a kitchen full of people while Molly prepared breakfast, Tammy wouldn't have to face Greg alone. Last night she'd faked a headache. Or at least Jude had said she had a headache and, bless him, he had brought her a tray of dinner.

Tammy had spent a sleepless night going over and over that kiss. She would love to blame Greg and say he was the one who kissed her, but that would be lying to herself. They had kissed each other, drawn in by some strange, invisible force that had tugged their lips together. Just like it had done the first time they'd ever kissed and then the two times after that when Tammy was eighteen. That was the day Greg asked her if he could take her to the prom. She sighed and walked out onto her balcony to stare at the mountains stretching in the distance as the sun peaked over them and rose slowly. The fresh country morning air filled her lungs, and the birds chirped with a promise of a bright sunny day.

Tammy had been up for two hours already. She'd showered and dressed for the day and was longing for a freshly brewed cup of coffee, but she couldn't risk bumping into Greg. Not right now anyway, when they would be on their own. Tammy was not ready to come face to face with him. They were supposed to work closely together and had done so for the past week without incident or once snapping at each other. After that kiss, Tammy was pretty sure things were going to be strained and awkward. One would think that Tammy was the queen of dealing with awkwardness, having been a rather awkward kid. But she'd worked hard to rise above that and become a confident adult woman. Well, that was until yesterday. One kiss from Greg Watson, and she was that awkward eighteen-year-old once again hiding out in her room until she knew it was safe to come out.

"Agghhh!!!" Tammy hissed. "Why does that man always seem to bring the worst out in me?"

She looked out over the mountains, once again wishing she had a warm cup of coffee in her hands to sip and enjoy the quiet – not that there was much quiet going on in her head right now, as thoughts of Greg kept echoing through it.

"I need to remember what he did and conjure up the anger again," Tammy spoke to the mountains as she used to do when she was a child. She used to think of them as stone giants that were her best friends and confidants. "Oh, goodness." She sighed. "How sad was I?"

She gave a self-mocking laugh, remembering how she used to stand on this balcony and talk to them.

"I guess that should show how sad I am. Because here I am talking to you again!" Tammy laughed. "Yup, one kiss from Greg, and I'm back to the Tammy that talks to the mountains." She turned and started walking towards her bedroom door. "That's it. I have to stop being a coward, go downstairs, and get a cup of coffee."

Tammy walked past her long mirror, stopped, backtracked,

turned, and looked at herself. She didn't have any make-up on. Since she got back to the ranch, Tammy rarely used it except for a touch of mascara. Her long, golden-blonde hair was neatly done into a French braid. Tammy would always wear it like that when she was younger. It stopped her hair from getting to knotted when she went riding. Tammy had a natural curl to her hair that became like a bird's nest at the slightest gust of wind. She usually wore it straight, but that took a lot of flat ironing. On humid days, Tammy's hair was also braided, or it'd just puff up like a dandelion.

Today Tammy had chosen to wear a light blue short-sleeved cotton shirt with snaps down the front. The top few buttons were open, allowing her shoulder blades to peep out. She wore no jewelry except for her watch. It was a gold Cartier that used to belong to her mother and was the only watch Tammy had ever owned. Her shirt was neatly tucked into her faded bootlegged denim with a dark brown leather belt and a small silver buckle through the waistband. The cuffs of her jeans hid the tops of her well-worn leather ankle boots. Today, Tammy looked like a more mature version of what she'd looked like when she was a teenager. She was no longer a stick figure but a slender, well-curved woman who kept herself in good shape.

Tammy hated running. Instead, she spent forty to fifty minutes every morning on her elliptical machine. It was much better than running, and with her large flat-screen TV, she could walk through any virtual terrain she liked. This morning, it had been the woods in the mountains with birds chirping and a beautiful waterfall. While she hiked through the virtual mountain path, her mind had been full of Greg Watson! If she was being honest, it had been full of Greg Watson since the day she'd arrived back home and found he was not only a guest in her house but its part-owner. Tammy stood staring at her reflection in the mirror, waiting for that burst of anger she got whenever she thought of having to share her home with him, but it wouldn't come.

"This is all his fault!" Tammy hissed to her reflection. "Why did he have to be so darn nice and honest about Brian's will."

Tammy couldn't even get cross at her uncle today for some reason. Instead, every time she thought about walking out her bedroom door, all she could think of was running into Greg. Her emotions did not react to that like she would like them to have. Over the past few days, when they'd been working together, she had found herself looking forward to seeing him. But she'd managed to keep those feeling under control and put them down to enjoying their detective work in looking into the avalanche at the ski resort. Today, she knew those feelings were about both their investigation and working alongside Greg.

"Oh no, Tammy!" Tammy whispered to her reflection. "You can't do this, girl." She dropped her head back and looked up at the ceiling. "Remember where having feelings for Greg Watson got you in the past."

A soft knock at her door had her head shooting around to look at it. Her heart fluttered, and she stood holding her breath, staring at the door.

"Aunt Tammy?" Brynn's soft voice called through the door. "Are you awake?"

"Yes, sweetheart," Tammy said, quickly shelving her emotional turmoil and rushing to her door. Something in Brynn's voice didn't seem right.

Tammy opened the door, her eyes widening when she saw Brynn's tear-stained cheeks.

"Oh, honey, what's wrong?" Tammy asked as Brynn threw her little arms around her waist and collapsed against her in tears.

"I miss my mommy and daddy," Brynn said through her sobs.

"Oh, sweetie." Tammy's heart broke for her niece.

Tammy wrapped her arms around the shaking child, leaned over, and closed her bedroom door. She led Brynn over to the bed where she sat and pulled Brynn onto her lap, holding her while she cried.

"I'm sorry," Brynn whispered through her ragged breaths.

"Never be sorry about how you feel, honey," Tammy told her.

She held Brynn's head against her chest with one hand and placed the other around her waist, rocking her gently. "You're going to have these moments, and when they come, we will ride them out together."

"I just feel so silly." Brynn sniffled.

"Brynn, you lost your parents, and they were a part of you," Tammy said gently.

"Do you feel like this?" Brynn asked Tammy, cuddling into her.

"I do!" Tammy admitted. "When I was young, I lost my mom. I used to do the same thing you're doing now. Whenever I had a sad moment, my dad would cuddle me in his lap, and we'd sit remembering her together. He told me that while the wound inside was healing, there would be moments when something opens it up again." She kissed Brynn's soft head. "But it eventually heals over and leaves a scar, which becomes a bittersweet memory."

"Does it still hurt after all this time?" Brynn sniffed.

"It's more like an ache and a longing to be able to get a hug from them," Tammy told her honestly. "Like now, I could really use my big brother. He was always there when I needed him." Tammy felt her throat start to burn and bit back the tears. "He could be so irritating at times, but he was my rock."

"I know, he could be so silly!" Brynn gave a watery laugh. "Mom would just roll her eyes and shake her head."

"I used to do that to him too." Tammy laughed. "I guess his bad big brother jokes became corny dad jokes."

"They did." Brynn laughed. "I miss his cloud-shaped pancakes."

"Oh, my goodness. Did he still make those?" Tammy shook her head, and her heart warmed as she heard Brynn giggle.

"He did." Brynn wiped her tears from her cheeks.

"You know he only called them cloud pancakes because he was hopeless at making round pancakes, right?" Tammy grinned when Brynn sat back to look at her. She was smiling again.

"Yes, I know." Brynn wiped more tears from her cheeks. "But

they were always delicious because mom said they were filled with all his love."

"They were." Tammy had to bite her lip to stop her eyes from misting over her eyes.

"Do you think you and I could make cloud pancakes one morning?" Brynn looked into Tammy's eyes.

"Of course," Tammy said. "Hey, why don't we go downstairs and make them now?"

"Really?" Brynn's eyes widened in delight.

"I think cloud pancakes are on the breakfast menu today." Tammy laughed when Brynn jumped off her lap, took her hand, and helped her stand.

"We'd better hurry before Aunt Molly starts breakfast," Brynn advised her.

"I have noticed how possessive she's become in the kitchen," Tammy said. She let Brynn lead her by the hand out of her bedroom, down the stairs, and into the kitchen.

The smell of freshly brewed coffee hit Tammy's senses and made her mouth water. A pair of green-gold eyes met hers, making her heart do crazy things in her chest and weak in the knees.

"Hi, Uncle Greg, Aunt Tammy and I want to make cloud pancakes," Brynn told him excitedly, blissfully unaware of the tension between Greg and Tammy.

"No way," Greg's eyes slid from Tammy's to Brynn's, and a warm smile spread across his absurdly handsome face. "You mean like your father's famous cloud pancakes?"

"Yup!" Brynn nodded.

"Are you sure your Aunt Tammy is the best one to try to make those?" Aunt Molly's voice was the most welcome voice Tammy had heard in ages.

"Oh, right!" Brynn said, and they immediately looked apologetically up at Tammy. "Uh..."

"It's okay, sweetheart." Tammy sighed. "I admit that maybe Aunt Molly would need to help us."

"Aunt Tammy, I think you make the best cheese and ham sandwiches." Brynn hugged her.

"Why, thank you," Tammy said, hugging Brynn back and kissing the top of her head. "Do you hear that, Aunt Molly?"

Tammy grinned, looking up at Molly, only to find she'd walked off, and Greg was standing in her place. Her grin froze on her face as their eyes locked and held. Tammy swallowed as her body started to feel like it was melting beneath his smoldering look.

*Uh oh, this is not good, Tammy!* She berated herself. *Get a grip, get a grip, get a grip!* She screamed silently to herself and dragged her gaze away from his.

"Why don't we go and help Aunt Molly?" Tammy took Brynn's hand and led her to the pantry, where Molly was taking out the pancake ingredients.

"I need to go and make sure the roster for today is ready," Greg said before excusing himself and leaving.

As soon as Tammy heard the back door close, she silently breathed in relief. *Coward!* Her subconscious said. *Better a happy chicken than a broken-hearted fool!* Tammy sneered at her subconscious and ruthlessly pushed any resurfacing feelings down. *No more thoughts of Greg and that mind-shattering kiss!*

<br>

Tammy had managed to avoid Greg for the remainder of the morning and left the ranch as soon as she could to go meet Ashley, Cat, Maria, and Chelsea. She parked her car in the parking space in the car park outside Cuthbert Law offices in Lewistown. Tammy got out of her car, and before she could clear the car park, she found Cat.

"Hi, Tammy," Cat greeted her.

"Hello, Cat," Tammy greeted her back. "Where are Maria and Chelsea?"

"They're sitting this one out," Cat told her. "I waited for you so we could walk to Ashley's father's house together."

"Why didn't we just park at his house?" Tammy frowned.

"Long story," Cat said with a big grin. "You'll soon find out why. Ashley is overly cautious about security these days."

"I'm not following you..." Tammy's frown deepened.

"Don't worry. It will all become clear soon enough." Cat laughed as she led the way to Ashley's father's house.

"I thought Ashley's parents lived near Holly's bakery?" Tammy looked at the neat two-story townhouse a road away from the law offices.

"Oh, Holly and Uncle Rupert are separated," Cat explained.

"Really?" Tammy was surprised.

"Yes." Cat sighed. "I was also shocked when I heard. They were so perfect for each other."

"Just goes to show you that even the most perfect couple isn't that perfect." Tammy sighed. "I once thought I had the perfect marriage. Turns out it was a controlling, lying, manipulative one. I was just too naïve to notice." She gave a self-mocking laugh. "To think I was this hot shot cleaner to the stars cleaning up all their messes while keeping their images squeaky clean. I could spot a lie or cheat from a hundred miles away. When it wasn't in my own life, that is."

"I know how you feel," Cat told her. "I was exactly the same with Paul." She linked her arm through Tammy's comfortingly. "You think everything is perfect because your husband showers all this attention on you, but it's just a cover-up for his indiscretions."

"Exactly," Tammy agreed. "I know it was not exactly the same. But I also know what it's like to be stolen from and used as my ex never signed the divorce papers. Instead, he held them off so he could milk my name to get himself a house, car, clothes, and a huge line of credit."

"No!" Cat's eyes widened. "I'm so sorry, Tammy, I didn't know that."

"It's not common knowledge, although I feel like everyone will know if it gets out that the avalanche that took my brother, his wife, and Martin's life was orchestrated," Tammy said, shocking Cat.

"Are you serious?" Cat stopped, let go of Tammy's arm, and stood staring at her in disbelief. "Who?" She stammered. "Why?" She frowned and shook her head. "Why would anyone want to do something so horrific?"

"We're not sure." Tammy looked at the ground as the pang in her heart for the loss of her brother shot through her.

"Come on, I think we have someone that may be able to help you find that out," Cat said with a sly smile.

"What do you mean?" Tammy's eyes narrowed suspiciously, wondering what the four of them had been up to.

"You'll have to wait and see," Cat told her. "I made a promise not to disclose this to anyone. Like you'll have to do before Ashley allows you to join us."

"Okay, now I'm really confused and suspicious." Tammy gave Cat a sideways glance but followed her to Rupert Cuthbert's new rental home. "Nice!" She said, looking at the two-story townhouse.

"Uncle Rupert does like his comforts." Cat laughed, pulling Tammy up to the front door, where it flew open before they even knocked.

"Hi," Ashley greeted them. "Come in," she welcomed Tammy. "You'll need leave your car keys, and cell phone here."

She looked at Tammy's watch. "The watch can stay."

"Thank you!" Tammy put her keys and cell phone in the tub Ashley gave her.

Tammy watched as Ashley put all her items into a wall safe behind a painting. It felt good to be part of a group of friends. Tammy only ever had one friend, Freddy, who she had to remind herself to visit soon. He still lived in Lewistown but was married and had taken over his family's chemist. When she lived in LA, her only friend had been Brenda and her late husband, who turned out to be not her friend at all, but her emotional jailer. Tammy shook off the feeling of anger starting to boil in her stomach once again. She couldn't be mad with him now, but she could be disgusted with his girlfriend. Tammy still couldn't believe what she'd found out about Ursula the previous day.

"Okay that's it," Ashley said drawing Tammy from her thoughts as she replaced the painting that covered the safe. "We have to move. We are being waited for." She glanced at her wristwatch.

"By whom?" Tammy asked following Ashley and Cat. "And why do we have to leave our keys and phones behind?"

"Miss Overly Cautious insists we leave everything here in case we're being tracked or monitored," Cat explained.

"I still don't understand what this is all about." Tammy looked at the two pairs of eyes looking back at her.

"You will," Ashley promised. "Now, let's hit the road."

"Are we going on a trip?" Tammy pried.

"Just a short one," Cat told her as they walked into the garage and piled into a late model Mustang.

"Nice," Tammy said, looking around the immaculate interior of the car.

As they drove off heading towards the outskirts of town, Cat and Ashley explained Ashley's secret hideout and her work done for a government agency that required it. When they pulled into a storage unit, Tammy was surprised to see it was closed and locked from the inside. Once one of the lockers opened up, they found a staircase on the other side of the locker, leading into a tunnel and then into a high-tech office. Her surprise only grew when she saw Wallace, Jane, and Donavan, Jane's brother, waiting for them there.

"Welcome, Tammy," Wallace greeted her. "I'm sorry about all the secrecy, but we really do not know who to trust."

"I'm flattered that you trust me," Tammy told them, looking around the room. "I feel like I'm in some spy movie high-tech lab."

"It's cool, isn't it," Jane said excitedly before introducing the four women to her brother.

"I knew I liked you from the start," Cat said to Jane. "How are you and Indy doing?"

"Cat!" Ashley hissed. "This is not the time to pry into your son's love life." She shook her head. "You shouldn't be prying at all."

"Really, 'Miss Super Spy' – when it comes to your children's love life?" Cat raised her eyebrows at Ashley.

"Tammy, Wallace told me about your interview with the FBI yesterday," Ashley brought up the previous day's interview. That Interview brought up as memories of what happened after it.

"Oh yes." Tammy looked at Jane. "I was interrogated by Jane's father."

"Oh!" Ashley couldn't suppress a shudder. "Sorry, Jane, but I've met him, and he can be a bit daunting."

"Yeah," Donovan agreed. "Tell me about it. I've had to live with him my entire young life."

"My condolences," Ashley said before turning back to Tammy. "If they want to talk to you again, call me right away."

"I will," Tammy promised. "My uncle was there, though, and I knew you had something to do."

"I know your uncle is an excellent lawyer, Tammy," Wallace said. "But Ashley is the one you need for anything regarding the avalanche or finding out what is going on with the ranches."

"Especially as your uncle is now representing Constance," Ashley looked sympathetically at Tammy.

"You know about Constance?" Tammy frowned.

"We do," Cat and Ashley said together.

"We are all shocked by it," Chelsea shook her head.

"It was a huge shock," Tammy admitted. "I still haven't quite got my head around it."

"Well, let's try and get all this trouble sorted out." Ashley moved towards the back of the room and picked up a small remote before taking a seat in the small living area in front of a huge monitor. "Please, come sit down."

Cat, and Wallace walked over to the area. Cat and Tammy sat on one of the sofas and Wallace in an armchair.

"Tammy, you started to tell us something about an accident

that nearly took the lives of West, Zac, and Brett," Ashley began the conversation.

"I did," Tammy recalled. "Is that why I'm here?"

"Oh no, not only because of that," Cat assured her. "We'd like to get to know you better. As neighbors, it would be nice for all of us to be good friends."

"I could really use some of those right now," Tammy smiled. "What do you want to know about the accident?" She looked at Ashley with a frown. "Why do you want to know about it?"

"To get to the bottom of the trouble in the ranches, we think we need to go back to when the trouble actually started," Wallace explained.

"I can remember some of the first incidents around our ranch starting when I was fifteen," Cat told her. "Maria told me that her family's started a few months after her parents' light aircraft accident."

"That was also the year all Chelsea's dogs were poisoned," Ashley reminded Cat. "It was the beginning of much of the other livestock on the Hitchins ranch getting poisoned."

"That's right," Cat remembered.

"I found some of my father's old papers, and there were a lot of death threats to him that year." Ashley's eyes narrowed thoughtfully. "It was also when Holly's bakery was being vandalized at least twice a month."

"It was also the year my father started dating my step-monster, Winnie Larson." Cat's eyes narrowed angrily.

"Yes!" Ashley clicked her fingers. "That's right."

"You don't think that she is behind this?" Cat looked at them aghast. "I know we suspected her before because she was Harris' aunt. He was the former foreman at Cupids Bow Ranch."

"They were both terrible people," Ashley shuddered.

"My father was filing for divorce, unbeknownst to us all, a few weeks before he was killed," Cat told them. "According to Chelsea, Ron Hicks, old man Donaldson's grandson, was the last man to see my father alive."

"Wouldn't Ron Hicks have been about the same age as David

and Zac then?" Wallace asked. "I think he is actually two years older than them."

"Yes, but he wasn't the only one in the stables at the time," Cat reminded them. "Chelsea also ran into Winnie, the step monster, on her way out."

"How would she have been able to knock your father off his horse, though?" Ashley looked thoughtful. "He was twice her size."

"She could've spooked his horse," Tammy suggested.

"You're right," Cat said. "King Callum, my father's horse at the time, never liked her."

"Where is this conversation going?" Ashley stopped their trip down memory lane.

"There seems to be a pattern," Cat explained. "Not sure if it means anything, but soon after my father announced he was marrying Winnie, the trouble stopped."

"I'm sure that must just be a coincidence." Ashley looked over at Cat.

"I think it's worth looking into." Wallace wrote in the notepad he'd pulled from his pocket. "Solving this is in all the details, which, as you know, we are missing a lot of."

"When did Winnie first make her appearance back in town?" Ashley asked Cat.

"A few months after my fifteenth birthday." Cat shrugged. "I'm not too sure."

"I'm sure she was connected with Bronwyn's dad's affair somehow." Tammy tried to recall some of the rumors about Winnie circulating when she was eighteen. "I think she was also somehow related to Greg."

"Yes, she is," Cat told her. "She's his father's sister."

"His aunt?" Tammy choked. "So that awful Harris man I've heard about is Greg's cousin because his mother would be Greg's father's sister?"

"Yes," Ashley said, her eyes flashing with anger. "He's had it out for all of us since he came to Lewistown."

"He's one of the reasons Chelsea and I had a falling out when we were seventeen." Cat's eyes became shadowed with sadness.

"I'm glad he's gone," Tammy smiled warmly at Cat.

"So, what you are all saying is that your families have a lot more than just one enemy?" Jane said from behind them.

"Or maybe they are all connected?" Wallace's eyes narrowed. "You think the trouble started when Cat, Chelsea, and Ashley were fifteen! That would've been around the same time Winnie Larson came back to town."

"Yes, but we bumped into Winnie before we went away for that show jumping competition in April." Cat's brows creased in thought.

"Most of the trouble we can remember started around October or November that year." Ashley's eyes widened as the memories came back to her. "Can you send a message to my father from me?" Ashley looked at Donovan. "I don't have my phone, and I know your tech boffs have a way of doing everything."

"Sure," Donovan said. "What do you want me to say?"

"Ask him if he remembers when exactly Callum Sparrow started to date Winnie Larson." Ashley's eyes narrowed in contemplation. "I think Wallace may be onto something about Winnie."

"What are you thinking?" Tammy asked her curiously.

"When I was going through Chelsea's mother's medical records she kept, I found a paternity test for Harris Conway." Ashley stood up. "It didn't say who it was being tested against, but I'm sure the permission for it was signed off by Winnie Larson. Well, it was her initials on the form anyway."

"What were the results?" Tammy asked.

"As far as I could read, they were negative," Ashley found the document and pulled it out.

"Want me to see if I can find out more about it?" Jane offered.

"Yes, please." Ashley handed the document over to Jane.

"I know one person we could simply ask about it." Cat looked at Ashley.

"I don't think we want to get any of Winnie's family or Harris involved in this right now." Wallace stopped Cat's train of thought.

"I guess you're right," Cat agreed.

"So, our list of suspects so far are Winnie Larson, Harris Conway, the Hicks family, and Jason Brown." Jane read of the list she'd made.

"The Hicks family are after the collection of artwork and antiquities that they think my father hid for old man Donaldson." Cat looked at Jane.

"Oh, there is also that company name that keeps popping up." Jane tapped her pen on her notepad.

"Which is?" Tammy asked.

"Division Four." Jane sat back in her chair, chewing the tip of her pen.

"Does anyone know who owns Division Four?" Tammy looked at Wallace.

"We're still looking into that as it is a black hole of Shell Companies." Wallace shook his head.

"Interestingly, they were the company sponsoring Paul Lockran and Astrid Hove's engagement party that was meant to be held at Cupids Bow Ranch." Donovan clicked the big screen in front of them.

An image of a check made out to Paul appeared on the screen.

"They were also sponsoring his and Astrid's tv show's revival program." Jane looked over her brother's shoulder at his screen.

"Oh, we can add Paul and Astrid to the list of our enemies." Cat shook her head in disgust. "They seemed pretty intent of coming to Montana to cause trouble."

"I think put Ursula Duggal on there as well," Tammy advised them. "She's in cahoots with Jason Brown."

"Okay, then." Jane's eye widened. "We have a few more

enemies to look into." She tapped her pen on her lips. "What if everyone is connected to Jason Brown somehow?"

All eyes turned to Jane while a memory niggled at the back of Tammy's mind. One that she'd kept locked up in the darkest recesses of her memory banks as it was one that cut through her soul. Tammy looked up at the people sitting with her in the living space as Ashley sat back down after placing a tray ladened with beverages and snacks on the coffee table. A painful knot twisted in Tammy's gut, and as much as she would like to keep that memory locked away forever, she knew it might be vital to their investigation. Her new friends needed to know what she knew about Jason Brown. Or at least what she thought she knew about him. To do that, Tammy had to revisit one of the most horrible and painful nights of her life for many different reasons.

"I think I may know Jason Brown's connection to all this!" Tammy's voice was barely louder than a whisper as she forced the words out.

All eyes turned to her in surprise. A silence descended over the room as everyone stared at her expectantly.

"It has to do with the night of mine, Zac's, and Brett's senior prom!" Tammy swallowed as she watched the interest in everyone's eyes intensify. "Before I begin to tell you, I have to say that this was possibly the worst night of my life."

# Chapter Two

# A PROM NIGHT TO FORGET

"Tammy, you don't have to do this!" Cat reached over and took her hand companionably, giving it a gentle squeeze.

"No, I have to," Tammy told her. "If Greg and I are ever going to get along or live side by side, I have to start making peace with what happened that night and take responsibility for the part I might have played in that dreadful accident. An accident that left a man in a wheelchair and nearly ended a lot of others dear to us all." She sucked in a shaky breath. "You have no idea what that night cost all our families and others."

"The night that has been erased from all the town's records and no one will talk about!" Ashley said softly. "We found some police reports about that night, but they were not much help." Her eyes suddenly grew wide. "Was that the mysterious Grayson that ended up in a wheelchair?"

"No, it wasn't Grayson who lost the use of his legs." Tammy shook her head, frowning. "I'm not even sure who Grayson is. Only that no one talks about him. I'm not even sure why West didn't want me to talk about Grayson Wyatt to Maria."

Jane looked over at Tammy, "Don't worry, we'll try and find out more about the man."

"I wish we could find that picture of Grayson Wyatt that

Aunt Simone had." Cat bit her lip. "I'm now more convinced than ever that he has something to do with this."

"I have to second your thoughts on that," Ashley backed Cat up. "Why would those pictures suddenly disappear?"

"Who else had access to my aunt's—" Cat suddenly stopped and looked at Maria. "Zac and Brett!"

"Yes, you said they went to Nashville for Simone's funeral." Ashley's eyes widened as she remembered. "They went through her things as Zac wanted some memorabilia of hers."

"Zac must have them at Cupids Bow." Wallace's eyes narrowed. "I'll get one of my men to have a scout around for them." He got up and walked off to contact one of his men.

"You never met anyone named Grayson that night of your prom?" Ashley asked Tammy, who shook her head. "If you're sure you want to tell us about that night, there might be something in your story that can point us to that man."

"Yes, I'm sure." Tammy swallowed. "I don't want to, but I know I need to tell the story. But remember, I can only tell you what I know and witnessed about that night."

"I'm sure that will be more than the pieces we currently have to put the puzzle together." Cat patted Tammy's hand.

Tammy gave them a small smile, gathering her thoughts and swirling emotions as she sent herself back in time to that horrible night.

## THIRTY-SEVEN YEARS AGO

Tammy was over the moon with happiness. She couldn't believe that Greg Watson had offered to take her to her senior prom. Constance had helped her pick out the most gorgeous dress that made her look like a princess. Tammy and Constance had spent the entire afternoon getting their hair and nails done. Constance would help Tammy with her makeup once she got dressed.

Tammy looked at her bedside clock. She only had another

hour, and then Greg would be here to pick her up. Tammy's heart pounded in her chest once again, and she touched her hand to her lips. Greg had kissed her after he asked her if he could take her to the prom. She sighed and flopped down on her bed, thinking about her very first kiss. Tammy had always secretly been in love with Greg, her older brother's best friend. Greg and her brother had been back from college for just over eight weeks now, and Tammy had seen Greg every day since then.

Greg was stabling his horse with them and came to ride it with Brian every day. Some days he would stay the night, and they would include Tammy when they sat around the fire pit making s'mores. She didn't know if it was her imagi-nation, but Greg would always make sure to sit next to Tammy every chance he got. If they went riding together, he'd keep pace with her and make sure she was alright while the rest of the group galloped off. Tammy was convinced that Greg felt the same way about her as she saw how he looked at her. It was different. More intense. And his body language, according to Vogue, suggested he had feelings for her too.

"Tammy, honey?" Constance knocked on her door. "It's time to start getting ready."

"Thank you, Constance," Tammy called back. "I'll let you know when I have showered and changed."

"Watch your hair in all that steam," Constance warned her. "Be sure to use the cap I got for you."

"I will." Tammy giggled, thinking about wearing that silly shower cap that made her look like a mushroom.

Once Tammy finished showering and getting dressed, she stood in front of her full-length mirror, staring at her reflection. She couldn't believe what a difference a beautiful dress could make to one's appearance. A knock at her door made her turn away from her mirror.

"Come in," Tammy said, unable to help the happiness and excitement from spilling into her voice.

"Oh, sweetheart!" Constance stood staring at her with misty eyes. "You look so much like your mother."

"Thank you," Tammy's voice dropped to a whisper. A lump formed in her throat at the thought of her mother. "I feel like a princess."

"Well, let's finalize your princess look then, shall we?" Constance wiped her eyes and grinned.

When Constance finished with Tammy, she looked even more like a princess. She didn't have a lot of makeup on. Constance had put a thin line of eyeliner on her lids to accentuate her eyes. A few strokes of mascara plumped and lengthened her already long, thick lashes. A soft gold dusted the rest of her eyelids, highlighting her big blue eyes. A soft, peachy pink touched up her high cheekbones, giving her a delicate blush while her full lips sparkled with gloss. Tammy's thick golden blonde hair was pulled up in a soft-knotted bun at the back of her head. Golden tendrils dipped down over her ears. Her fringe parted to the side, and parts of it gently touched her face.

"Gorgeous!" Brian's voice came from her door, making her spin around. "You look just like mom."

"Thank you!" Tammy smiled at her older brother. "Where are you going all dressed up?"

"We're going to Crazy Watts place for a party," Brian told her. "I think Greg was planning on bringing you after the prom, but now I'm not so sure I want all those guys ogling my beautiful sister." He grinned.

"I don't think you should be going to any parties either, young lady." Constance gave her a withering look. "You know your daddy will be a chaperone at the prom tonight."

"I know!" Tammy leaned over and kissed Constance on the cheek. "Besides, you know I'm not the party type."

"That's a relief to your big brother." Brian walked into the room and gave her a kiss on her head. "Behave yourself tonight and make sure that friend of mine does as well."

"We all know Greg only offered to take me because you probably told him to." Tammy smiled up at her brother.

"Nope," Brian denied. "I actually tried to stop him from asking you out." He looked down at his sister. "The last thing I want is my sister falling for a Watson."

"Why?" Tammy frowned.

"Because you have bigger things in your future than getting stuck in this small town," Brian told her. "Greg's future is here. Once his father retires, he'll probably be the one to take over the business." He laughed. "Everyone knows his crazy sister or irresponsible brother can't do it."

Tammy frowned up at Brian, but before she could ask him anything else, the doorbell rang. Her heart lurched as she knew who would be standing on the other side of it. All thoughts of Brian's conversation vanished from her head as thoughts of Greg and their evening ahead flooded her mind. She wanted to race down the stairs, swing the door open, and have him pull her into his strong arms. But his brother beat her to the door, and she nearly tumbled down the last few stairs when she saw Greg step inside.

He looked even more handsome in his tuxedo. Her heart was hammering so loudly in Tammy's chest when he turned to look at her. Their eyes locked and held, making Tammy's knees weak. Her legs were so shaky at the look in his eyes that she nearly missed the last step. Luckily, Constance was next to her and steadied her before she made a complete fool of herself by landing flat on her face.

"You look gorgeous," Greg's voice sounded a little gruff, and the black look Brian gave him didn't go unnoticed by Tammy. "This is for you." He held up a corsage.

"Thank you," Tammy smiled shyly at him and took the flower from him.

Their fingertips brushed and sent a jolt of electricity to her already pounding heart.

"Here, let me help you with that." Brian stepped between Tammy and Greg.

Brian took the box, pulled out the flower, and slipped it onto her wrist.

"Can the two of you please pose for me?" Constance dashed past Tammy to get the camera she'd left on the side table by the door. "This is a memory to keep."

Tammy could barely remember the camera light flashing in her eyes after Greg stepped up next to her and put his arm around her. She barely recalled Constance draping the soft floor-length cape around her shoulders. Tammy felt like she was walking on clouds while her soul played the music of love that her heart was happily dancing to.

On the drive to Lewistown, Greg kept the conversation light and spoke to her about horses as they sat side by side in the limousine, he'd hired for them while sipping sparkling grape juice. Tammy didn't need champagne or alcohol to feel giddy. Just being so close to Greg was having that effect on her. When they got to the prom and Tammy walked in on the arm of Greg Watson, she knew she was the envy of every girl there. Most of them couldn't believe their eyes when they saw who her partner for the dance was. Greg told her that they were all looking at her because of how she'd transformed from the shy girl hiding in the corner to a beautiful swan.

The night was going so well, and Greg didn't let her out of his sight. He took away her nerves by making her laugh, covered her disastrous dance moves as he glided her across the floor, and took her for a moonlight stroll around the gardens when she felt overwhelmed. It was there that she and Greg shared their second kiss, and it was not like the first kiss. This kiss was deep and grew in intensity, making her giddy as she wanted to draw closer to him. Although it lasted a lot longer than their first kiss, it also ended too soon for Tammy. When he stepped away from her, she felt so cold she couldn't help the shudder that shook her shoulders.

"You're cold," Greg's voice was hoarse, and he cleared his throat. "Let's get you back inside. I think they are about to announce your prom king and queen." He grinned down at her, taking her small hand in his. "Come on." He pulled her back inside, holding her hand possessively.

Tammy was so happy she felt as if she would burst as she let Greg lead her back into the hall where everyone was gathering for the announcement. He pulled her through the crowd to the front, at the foot of the stage and next to the stairs leading up to it. Tammy's principal walked past them as she climbed the stair with an envelope in her hand. The previous year's king and queen followed the principal up the stairs, standing to one side as the principal walked up to the microphone.

"Good evening, students!" Mrs. Lowery smiled, and the crowd greeted her back.

Tammy felt Greg draw her closer to him until their arms were touching. She could smell his cologne, and it teased her senses. A smile spread across her lips as she glanced at the crowd. She felt so proud to be at Greg's side. For once, she wasn't the outcast who stood by the sidelines, fading into the background while everyone else shone. Tammy was so deep in thought that she almost missed the announcement.

"Your prom queen is..." Mrs. Lowery paused for dramatic effect, "Bronwyn Brown."

The crowd broke into cheers and applause while Tammy felt the knife rip through her happy bubble as Greg stiffened beside her. Her world was tilting, and her happiness started to leak out of her deflating bubble when she turned to see Bronwyn sashay towards them. She looked as gorgeous as ever in her form-hugging red dress. Her long blonde hair flowed loosely around her shoulders. When she brushed past them, Tammy was sure Bronwyn deliberately walked closer to Greg, stopping to whisper something in his ear, making his shoulders stiffen even more. Tammy glanced up at Greg, whose face had gone pale as his head turned to watch Bronwyn glide up the stairs.

When the prom queen collected her crown and took the

mic, her eyes moved to catch Tammy's. She could see what she thought was spite sparkle in Bronwyn's brown eyes before she glanced away to start her speech and accept her title. It wasn't any surprise that the school's quarterback was the prom king. When the king and queen took to the dance floor, a hush fell over the room, even if no one knew how much the king and queen actually hated one another. Them standing stiffly, glaring at each other was a dead giveaway. But they danced the customary dance and then couldn't let go of each other fast enough when it was over. When that dance ended, Tammy knew that her happy evening had ended with it when she'd seen that Greg had not taken his eyes off Bronwyn as they danced.

"Can you excuse me for a minute?" Greg let go of Tammy's hand and gave her an apologetic look before walking out of the hall.

Tammy's eyes glanced around the room just in time to see Bronwyn exit the hall too in the same direction that Greg went. Tammy felt her heart crack and ache, and her head spun with confusion. An image of the second day Greg was back from college flashed through her mind. Tammy was out with Freddy when she'd seen Greg at the diner with Bronwyn. They looked like they were arguing. But Freddy had distracted her with something and dragged her away. By the time they walked back past the diner, Greg and Bronwyn were gone. Tammy knew they used to be an item four years ago when Greg was still at school.

Greg and Bronwyn had supposedly broken up when Greg had graduated high school. But Tammy had seeing Greg and Bronwyn in the diner a couple of weeks ago. She'd asked her brother about it, but he'd said that Greg hadn't mentioned it to him. All Brian knew was that Greg and Bronwyn's break up all those years ago was mutual. Brian didn't really think the two of them were that serious about each other. But after witnessing what she had, Tammy didn't believe what Brian had said was true. There was definitely still something between the two of them, and Tammy was standing abandoned at her prom as the proof of it. Anger suddenly spurted through Tammy as she realized that Greg may have just used her to get into the prom hall to see Bronwyn. Tammy looked around the room and saw her father dancing with her principal as they watched the students on the floor. He looked like he was having a good time, and she didn't want to disturb him. Tammy decided to get herself some punch and calm down. Maybe she was overreacting, and Greg had simply gone to the bathroom. But as Tammy walked past a group of Bronwyn's friends, her anger turned to humiliation as she overheard what they said.

"Did you see how Greg just dropped Tammy to rush after Bronwyn?" One girl said and laughed.

"I always knew those two were meant for each other," another girl chipped in. "Did wallflower Tammy think just because she put on some makeup and an expensive dress, he'd be interested in the likes of her?"

The group of girls laughed.

"Good grief, no!" One of them said between laughs. "Bronwyn is like gold. Tammy is nothing but a lump of coal."

"It was so obvious that he only brought her here so he could get close to Bronwyn again," another girl added.

"Yes, I believe she turned him down when he begged her to let him bring her to the dance," the girl who had started the conversation said.

"Should we go and tell Tammy she may as well ask daddy to take her home because her date won't be returning?" They all laughed again.

Tammy's cheeks flamed with humiliation. Hot anger spurted through her, numbing the searing pain ripping through her soul and making her heart ache. As the girls' words echoed through Tammy's mind, her anger turned into a blinding rage. Before she knew what she was doing, she stormed towards the direction she'd seen Greg go. Tammy didn't know what she would do or say when she found him. All she knew was she wanted to find out if it was all true and see it for herself. Tammy stormed through the doors and headed out into the chilly night, looking for Greg. It didn't take her long to find them hiding behind an outbuilding, trying hard to keep their angry voices hushed.

Tammy didn't care if she looked like an enraged shrew as she marched toward them. All she could think of was how dare Greg, who'd known her since she was a baby, do this to her? Why wouldn't he tell her the truth? Why kiss her and make her feel like he did when he was only waiting to see Bronwyn? Why use her to get closer to Bronwyn? The more these thoughts circulated in her head, the angrier she seemed to get. When she drew closer and was about to make her presence known, she froze as she saw Greg's arms reach out and his hands circle Bronwyn's shoulders.

"What are you trying to tell me, Bron?" Greg hissed.

"I need help, I can't go through this on my own!" Bronwyn's words crashed through Tammy's anger like a bucket of icy water, leaving her shaking where she stood, gasping for air.

"When?" Greg's voice seemed to tear from his chest.

"You know when!" Bronwyn's voice was rough and filled with pain like she'd been crying.

"Bron..." Greg pulled her to him and stepped into Tammy's view as he wrapped his arms around Bronwyn. "Why didn't you come to me sooner? I warned you about this."

"I know!" Bronwyn sniffed into his chest. "I'm so sorry to have..." She stopped, and her eyes met Tammy's. "Tammy!" She pushed herself out of Greg's arms. Bronwyn's face paled as she looked into Tammy's eyes. "I..."

"Tammy!" Greg immediately stepped around Bronwyn and started to walk towards her.

"Don't!" Tammy put both her hands up to stop him. "So, what your gang of friends said was true." She fought to keep her voice steady and swallowed down the emotion burning her throat as her eyes narrowed on Bronwyn and then flew back to Greg. "You know you didn't have to pretend to be interested in me to get me to bring you to the prom." Her voice filled with scorn. "All you needed to do was tell me the truth."

"Tammy, you don't understand..." Greg tried to step toward

her, but she backed up, so he stopped. "I don't know what you heard just now."

"Enough!" Tammy told him, trying hard to conjure up the anger that had driven her there in the first place. "I think you've caused me enough humiliation and given her crew more fuel to make fun of me."

"Tammy, we…" Bronwyn tried to reach out to Tammy, but she shook her head.

"Stay away from me," Tammy warned Bronwyn. "And I suggest you tell your spiteful crew of pom-pom pushers to do the same, or you'll get to know the real me!"

Her eyes narrowed as the words of her friends once again went through her mind. The anger started to churn, pushing back the pain and threatening to break her into a heap of tears. Tammy would not give them the satisfaction of seeing her cry. She would hold her head up high as she always did. Tammy had no broken bones, and their words could only harm her if she let them. She was not going to let them do that to her anymore. Tammy's eyes fell on Bronwyn once again. Her eyes were puffy and red.

"I hope the two of you are very happy together," Tammy felt the sting of tears starting to burn her eyes.

"I…" Bronwyn looked at Tammy with a confused frown.

Tammy turned on her heel and was about to storm away.

"Tammy, please, wait!" Greg ran after her, grabbing her arm and spinning her around.

Another blaze of red-hot anger tore through Tammy, giving her a second chance at a few moments to hold onto her tears.

"Don't you dare touch me!" Tammy ripped her arm from his embrace as if he'd burned her. She tore a piece of the anger burning inside her. "If you ever come near me again, I'll make sure it's the last thing you do. I wish I'd never have to see your face again."

Greg stepped back. His face was pale with shock at her words. Greg stood staring at her like she'd just stabbed him in the heart and betrayed him, which only fed fuel to the fire inside of her.

Another thought swirled through Tammy's mind; *how dare he look at me like I'm the one who's done something wrong?* She stood looking at him, but she flinched once she saw his shock turn to a cold mask of indifference.

"Fine," Greg said softly and stepped back. "I'll honor your wishes." He glanced at the hall. "How are you going to get home?"

"Don't worry yourself about that," Tammy sneered nastily. "I'm sure you have much more pressing matters to worry about." Her eyes slid to where Bronwyn was standing, watching them.

With that, Tammy turned and stalked off, hoping he couldn't see how shaky her legs were or that her eyes didn't betray the pain slicing through her heart and ripping at her soul. She walked into the hall and went straight up to her father. Tammy ignored the side-long glances and snickering from Bronwyn's followers. She even let their comment about them – guessing they didn't have to rub it into Tammy's face after all – slide off her back.

At that moment, Tammy felt sorry for Bronwyn. Tammy may not have as many friends as her, but at least she could trust her friends with her secrets, and she knew she could rely on them. All Bronwyn really had was a group of hangers-on wanting to raise their social status by surrounding the most popular girl at school. Tammy walked up to her father.

"Daddy, could you take me home, please?" Tammy clenched her hands at her side, hoping her father couldn't see what was going on inside her. He'd always told her she had the most expressive eyes.

"Sure, pumpkin." Garth Anderson looked around the room. "Where's Greg?"

"He wanted to go to that party Brian and the rest of their group went to." Tammy was shocked at how easy that lie slipped out. "I don't want to go to any parties. You know that's not my scene."

"That's very responsible of you, honey," Garth said proudly. "Give me a few minutes, and I'll meet you at the car, okay?"

"Okay, I'll go get my cloak." Tammy turned to go towards the cloakroom when her eyes met Greg's.

He was also going towards the cloakroom. Tammy was the first to break eye contact and stiffened her shoulders. She would not let him intimidate her or stop her from getting her cloak. Tammy stalked over to the cloakroom and got there ahead of him. She asked for her cloak but remembered that Greg had her ticket when she was asked for it. A long arm reached over her and handed the woman in the booth three tickets. Tammy didn't say a word, nor did she turn around, but she was very aware of how close behind her he was.

"I'm asking you one last time to talk to me, Tammy, and let me explain," Greg said softly into her ear.

"There is nothing to explain," Tammy hissed, grabbing her cloak and stepping around him. "I think I heard more than enough, and I don't want to hear the details."

"I seem to recall the last time you came in on the tail end of a conversation," Greg grabbed her arm, not letting her walk off.

He turned and took the two coats with his free hand before pulling her to the one side away from the booth. Tammy noticed he'd gotten his coat and a woman's too, which she presumed was Bronwyn's. She felt the pain rising again and knew she needed to get as far from him as possible. But his grip on her arm was holding her firmly to him.

"Do you remember how much trouble you got Brian into because you wouldn't let him explain things to you?" Greg reminded her.

"I don't think I'm the one who's gotten anyone in trouble this time," Tammy looked at him, not caring that her mask of composure might be slipping. All she wanted was to get out of there and be away from him, Bronwyn, and all her spiteful cheerleader hangers-on. "I think this time that's all you."

A noise caught their attention, and his head snapped around.

His hand quickly dropped from her arm when they saw Tammy's father walk toward him.

"Ah, there you are," Garth said cheerfully, not noticing the tension between the two. "I hope you're not trying to convince my daughter to go with you to that party?"

"I beg your pardon, sir?" Greg looked at Garth, confused.

"It's okay. I asked my father to take me home because you wanted to go to the party Brian's at, and as you know, I hate parties." Tammy put on the most cheerful voice she could muster.

"Oh, right." Greg's eyes slid towards hers. She saw some emotion flicker in them, but it was gone before she could decipher it. "Well, I'd better get going." He looked at Garth. "Thank you for taking Tammy home." He leaned into Tammy. "Don't worry. I won't darken your door again. I hope you don't come tumbling down off that high horse of yours one day."

Tammy's eyes flew to his in shock at the anger in his voice, but he looked away from her. He smiled, shook hands with Tammy's father, and walked away.

"Holly has just told me she's staying open late tonight for all the parents that chaperoned the prom," Garth told Tammy once he retrieved his coat. "I think we should stop by and stuff ourselves with some of her tasty treats."

"Dad!" Tammy shelved the turmoil whirling inside her. When she was alone later that night, she'd let the storm break, but, for now, she had to put on a smile and enjoy some pie. "You know I should stop you because of your strict diet, but, heck, it's a special night so let's do it."

Three hours later, Tammy and her father were getting ready to leave Holly's café. They'd spent the rest of the evening with Elaine Parker, Maria's grandmother, Dr. Denton Hitchin, Callum Sparrow, Rupert Cuthbert, Samantha, and William Beckett. It always surprised Tammy that their families were supposed to be locked in some feud, but they would get together like they did on this night and have a good time. Garth and Tammy were just saying goodbye when Holly got a call at the café. It was Dr.

Hitchens's wife calling. Dr. Debbie Hitchin said there'd been an accident, and she needed them all at the hospital as fast as they could get there.

As most of them tumbled out of the door, Dr. Debbie Hitchin asked to speak to Rupert. When they arrived at the hospital, it was to learn that Brian, Greg, Zac, Brett Parker, West, Bronwyn, and their friend Watts were in a serious accident. Watts had been driving, and his blood alcohol was just over the limit. The night seemed to drag on endlessly, and so did the weeks that followed. Everyone who had been in the car was seriously injured except Bronwyn. Some even more alarming news was that Bronwyn's father had been almost fatally wounded in the accident. Tammy wasn't sure of the details, and no one ever told her.

All she could gather was that Bronwyn's father had run out into the middle of the road straight into the van Tammy's brother and friends were in. Watts had tried to swerve, but Bronwyn's father had jumped at the vehicle and got run down as it hit a pole. He'd broken his spine in a few places and became paralyzed from the waist down. Bronwyn never returned to school after that night, and no one heard of her or her mother again. When her father passed away five months later, neither Bronwyn nor her mother attended the funeral.

# Chapter Three

# REPEATING MISTAKES

*P*resent Day

As Tammy returned to the present day, she realized that her cheeks were wet with tears, and her throat felt raw with emotion. She knew going back over that night and time would burst the wound she'd ignored for all these years. Tammy felt drained and vulnerable, having spilled it all out, but she also felt free like a heavy weight had been lifted off of her.

"Oh, my word, Tammy." Cat's voice was wobbly, and her eyes misted with tears while her cheeks were wet with the ones that had spilled while Tammy had told her story.

Tammy looked around the room to see there was not a dry eye. Even Wallace's eyes were suspiciously watery.

"How dare Greg do that to you?" Ashley wiped her cheeks. Anger sparked in her eyes. "I can't understand how thoughtless some people can be."

"Then he had the audacity to give you one last chance to let him explain!" Cat shook her head in disgust.

"I wonder what happened to Bronwyn Brown and her mother?" Wallace looked thoughtful. "You don't think that Jason Brown is Bronwyn's son?"

"I think Bronwyn had a brother." Tammy frowned as she tried to recall his name. "He was in the same class as us, so he must've been only about eleven months to a year younger than her." She looked thoughtful. "But if I remember his name, was Winston. Jason is his son?"

"Now, if we had your yearbook, we could see what he looked like," Cat said.

"I do have a yearbook," Tammy saw the surprise on their faces when she said that. "Everyone got a yearbook that year."

"We can't find any traces of it," Cat told her. "No one will even talk to us about your prom night or the accident we discovered only recently."

"We were all away at a horse show," Ashley explained to Tammy. "When we got back Cat was told her brother had been in a football accident."

"That was the same year Harris came to Lewistown." Cat's brows drew together. "His aunt and him getting to town around the same time couldn't be a coincidence."

"Harris only arrived near the end of that year, though," Ashley pointed out.

"The first incidents only started mid to end of that year," Cat reminded them.

"Your father messaged back," Donovan told Ashley. "He said that, as far as he remembers, it was about September or October thirty-seven years ago that Callum started dating her."

"None of this makes sense." Tammy shook her head. "Is it possible Jason Brown is coming after our ranches and family because he feels they were to blame for Bronwyn's father's accident that must've contributed to his death five years later?"

"Maybe he was Jason's grandfather?" Cat suggested. "But why would Bronwyn and her mother just disappear?" She looked at Tammy. "Did her brother disappear as well?"

"No," Tammy shook her head. "He was at school right up until graduation."

"I think we've found out who Jason Brown is," Jane grabbed their attention. "Winston got married and had a son name Jason who's age fits with Jason Brown's."

"So, this is a Brown vendetta?" Cat's brow creased.

"Wait a minute," Jane said. "This is odd. I've just found Winston Brown's birth certificate. He was only seven months' younger than Bronwyn."

"How on earth is that even possible?" Ashly's face crumpled in confusion.

"Because he didn't have the same mother as Bronwyn," Jane said. "His mother is listed as Winnie Larson." Jane slid down in her chair as she watched the shock widen everyone's eyes.

"No way," Cat chocked. "So, Winnie came after my family for what?" She shook her head. "To get revenge?"

"And get this." Jane sat back up. "I found evidence that Bronwyn's mother was filing for divorce the year she and Bronwyn disappeared." Jane put the papers up on the screen. "She claimed her husband was having an affair, and that she was a victim of domestic violence."

"Where are you getting all this information from?" Ashley looked over at the brother and sister.

"Your father's files," Jane told her honestly. "It also looks like all the money the Browns had belonged to Bronwyn's mother and not the father. She cleaned out her bank account the day she and Bronwyn disappeared."

"So, we've all become targets because a domestic dispute between the Browns may have led to Bronwyn and her mother's disappearing?" Cat said in disbelief. "I don't understand how that would've had anything to do with any of our families."

"I don't it's because of that. It could have something to do with the accident instead!" Ashley asked. "That accident put Bronwyn's father in a wheelchair, and he died not long after that." She looked at Jane. "Did you manage to find anything at all on Bronwyn and her mom from after that night?"

"Nothing," Jane told them. "It just seems a bit much that Jason Brown blew up a mountain to cause an avalanche to take out his enemies because of some vendetta against his step-mother and sister." She shook her head. "But if he is behind what's been happening on the ranches, there has to be a deeper reason. That is more like a cat and mouse game going on long before he was born."

"Maybe he's carrying out a vendetta passed down to him by his father and Winnie?" Cat explained.

"I just think we're missing something," Jane told them. "What he's doing seems fueled with hate and revenge. There must be more to it than what we're seeing. I'll keep digging."

"I don't mean to go over your story," Ashley looked at Tammy apologetically. "But you said that someone called Watts was driving the car that night. You also mentioned your brother going to his party. Could he be the WW on the accident report?"

"It could be." Tammy frowned. "I never met him."

"You also mentioned in your story that Greg had a brother?" Wallace looked at Tammy questioningly.

"I never met him either. I think he lived in Billing with Greg's mother due to some sort of disease he had and had to live near a place equipped with medical facilities to help him." Tammy answered Wallace. "Greg hardly mentioned him or his mother, although I do know he visited Billings a lot."

"We'll look into that!" Jane promised. "Maybe Watts is short for Watson?"

"Could be!" Tammy turned to look at Jane. "Like I said, I never met either of them."

"Who do you think the other passenger was?" Ashley asked. "Could it have been Bronwyn's mother?" Her eyes widened. "Maybe they were helping them escape?" She looked at Cat. "Why would they have Chelsea's parents' van?"

"I don't know." Cat shook her head. "We'd have to ask Chelsea and see is she knows anything about someone having an accident in it around that time."

"Tammy, what do you think Greg wanted to explain to you about Bronwyn?" Ashley turned her interrogation on Tammy. "What did he mean about coming into the tail end of a conversation?"

"I once heard Greg and my brother talking about drugs." Tammy sighed. "All I heard was selling the drugs would make a lot of money. I was so shocked I immediately ran and told Constance, who, in turn, told my father. Needless to say, there was a big hoo-ha about it."

"Ah!" Ashley nodded. "Did you ever stop to think that what Greg meant that night was that what you heard may not have been what you thought it was?"

"Uh..." Tammy was speechless at the thought.

No, she hadn't thought of it that way at all. Instead, she'd thought of it as him looking for excuses so she wouldn't tell her brother or father what he'd done or about Bronwyn.

"What if Bronwyn was only asking Greg with his help to get away from her father?" Ashley threw some more kindle into the sparking flames of doubt she was igniting inside of Tammy. "I take it you never spoke to him again after that night?"

"No, by the time he'd recovered, I'd already decided to go to university in California," Tammy told them. "While I was scouting out universities in LA, I met Martin, and we all know the rest of that story."

"So, you never had contact with Greg again until you came home a few weeks ago?" Ashly looked at Tammy with narrowed eyes.

"Yes, that's correct." Tammy felt like she was in the witness box of a courtroom.

"Tammy, I'm on your side," Ashley assured her. "But I'm going to play devil's advocate here and say you need to start listening to the other side of a story. Although I'm once again completely on your side, I do think you and Greg need to sort this out."

"I agree!" Wallace said. "I'm not much of a romantic. All I know about love I've only just recently learned with Janine." He turned beet red as all the women 'ahhhed' him. He cleared his throat. "I've seen the way the two of you look at each other and trust me, I have never seen Greg look at another woman like he looks at you – not even his ex-wife."

"How long have you known Greg for?" Tammy quickly shifted the subject.

"A long time," was all Wallace would say.

"Boy, you're nearly as good as Maria at dodging questions about emotional things." Cat laughed. "Tammy, it's as clear as day that the two of you still have feelings for each other and a lot of unresolved issues."

"Until we can find out where Bronwyn disappeared to and what happened to her and her mother," Ashley advised. "I think you need to give the man the benefit of the doubt and go talk to him."

"Well, it's kind of awkward at the moment." To her mortification, Tammy felt her cheeks heat up.

"Something happened, didn't it?" Ashley's shrewd eyes narrowed on Tammy.

"It was just a kiss!" Tammy blurted out and felt her cheeks grow even hotter.

"Is that why you wanted to meet earlier?" Cat guessed. "You were trying to run away and avoid him!" She grinned. "Don't worry. I'm not judging you."

"No, because it's exactly what you do!" Ashley pointed out to Cat.

"There are still a lot of secrets that we don't know." Cat turned the subject away from her love life. "Like what are Zac, West, Brett, and Greg hiding about the night of the prom and the accident? She looked at Tammy. "At least, thanks to Tammy, we now know more about it than we could find before."

"I think we should go and find out!" Wallace said, staring at his phone.

"How?" Tammy asked. "Are we just going to gather them together and ask them straight out?"

"We don't need to gather them together." Wallace started to stand up. "They are already meeting not too far away from here in that new fancy housing development. It is also not the first time they've met there this past month."

"Who lives there?" Cat asked looking up at Wallace curiously.

"Someone called G. W. Watson." Wallace turned his phone.

"Who – according to my man who's been trailing your brothers and Greg – goes by the name of Grayson Wyatt." His head shot up, and he looked at Tammy apologetically. "My other man just found the picture of your aunt with Grayson Wyatt."

"And?" Cat said impatiently.

Wallace glanced at Cat before turning back to Tammy. His eyes blazed angrily, "Maybe you were right about the man, after all."

"I don't understand." Tammy frowned as Wallace turned his phone around.

Everyone sitting in front of him gasped when they saw the handsome face with sandy brown hair and green-gold eyes staring back at them. His right arm was around Simone's shoulders, and the other around another woman's shoulders they all recognized.

"I guess we now know what happened to Bronwyn Brown!" Tammy hissed once again, feeling her world being tilted upside down while her heart was being ripped through by a hot arrow of betrayal.

"It's time for a showdown!" Cat's eyes narrowed angrily. "We are with you side by side, Tammy."

Ashley stood up calmly and eyed them out, "You all, need to calm down." She looked at each of them. "Remember, we still only know pieces of this puzzle. Pieces that we've gathered from bits of paper and one person's point of view."

"Ashley's right!" Jane came and stood beside Ashley. "You can't go in there with all guns blazing. You have the element of surprise here. They've been covering this up for a long time now, and if they're all gathering, they may know that their time is running out."

"You need to keep level heads and let me do the talking!" Ashley's eyes narrowed even more when Wallace tried to say something. "You do better at listening!"

"You're right." Wallace sighed. "Fine, I say we get in my van, and we take a drive over there, planning our strategy along the way."

"Donovan and I will stay here and see what else we can dig up." Jane walked back to her desk, opened the drawer, and pulled out a burner phone. "Tammy, this is for you."

"Uh, thank you." Tammy gave Jane a sideways look as she took the phone.

"No one can trace any calls you make," Jane explained.

"There's one more thing you ladies should know!" Donovan told them as they started to walk towards the door. "Someone else lives at the house you're going to."

All eyes turned to Donovan as he put the picture of Zac hugging a woman on the large screen. As soon as Tammy saw that picture, she felt her heart shattering into a million pieces. She no longer wanted to go with them to confront her past. Instead, she wanted to run and hide under her bed where the world couldn't find her as she finally broke down, letting all the pain bleed out of her in a river of tears.

"It's going to be okay!" Wallace put a strong arm around her shoulders, and soon she was sandwiched in a six-people hug.

"We will not let you fall or break!" Cat promised her.

"We all have your back, Tammy," Ashley gave her a warm, encouraging smile.

Tammy's throat clogged up with emotion as she looked at her new friends, and for the first time since she could remember, she didn't feel so alone. She felt safe as she drew on all the strength and love they had sent her way. Tammy straightened her shoulders, took a deep breath, and marched to Wallace's vehicle. She felt like a soldier marching to war with her most trusted allies beside her. Tammy knew her heart may be shattered, but she also knew she now had a support group who would help her piece it back together. As the vehicle took off, Tammy thought about what Ashley had said about letting Greg explain things before jumping to conclusions. There was always the possibility that she'd just jumped to another one. Tammy's mind snapped back to the kiss they'd shared the previous evening and knew that it had been filled with as much emotion from Greg as it had been from her.

*I'll give Greg the benefit of the doubt and hear him out!* Tammy promised herself, feeling a little better about the upcoming meeting.

y the time they'd pulled up at the gate of the housing development, Tammy was a bundle of nerves.

"I'm here to see Mr. Watson," Wallace told the security guard.

"Is he expecting you, sir?" The guard asked him.

"No, but if you call up to the house and tell him Wallace Black and some other familiar faces are here to see him about a prom," Wallace raised an eyebrow. "I'm sure he'll tell you to send us right up."

"One moment, please." The guard gave him a curious look, walked into his hut, and could be seen making a call. A few minutes later, he came back out and looked into the window. "You can go through. It's number two-three-seven."

"Thank you." Wallace waved to the guard and pulled off.

The closer they got to the house more nervous Tammy became, and by the time they got to the front door, she was afraid she wouldn't be able to walk. She felt like jello inside. When they all piled out of the car, the front door opened, and Greg appeared, looking very different in dress pants, a cotton shirt open slightly at the neck and handmade leather loafers. He looked like an elusive author instead of the cowboy she knew and... Tammy stopped that thought before it even entered her head.

"Who's at the door, darling?" A familiar voice made Tammy freeze as the perfectly groomed Bronwyn Brown stepped out and linked her arm possessively with Greg's.

Bronwyn's eyebrows raised as she scanned the six people standing in front of her. Her gaze stopped and widened when they landed on Tammy.

"Hello, Bronwyn." Tammy's voice was flat and devoid of

emotion as their eyes locked.

"Tammy!" Bronwyn's face paled. She dragged her eyes away from Tammy and looked up at Greg. "I think you need to invite our guests inside."

"I was just going to do that," Greg smiled lovingly down at Bronwyn.

Tammy felt Cat and Ashley stiffen, as she did, at the look Greg gave Bronwyn.

"Well, I never!" Cat hissed beneath her breath for their ears only. "I'm sorry, but I don't know if I'm going to be able to keep my cool."

"You have to!" Ashley warned Cat. "Remember Wallace told us that Zac, Brett, and West are here too."

"That doesn't make me any less angry," Cat said through her gritted teeth. "Are you okay?" Cat linked her arm through Tammy's. "Come on. You've got this."

"Do you mind if I just take a moment?" Tammy looked at Cat.

"Sure." Cat nodded, unlinked her arm, and walked toward the rest of the group.

Tammy watched them disappear into the house while Gregg stood back from the door, allowing them to enter. When they were all inside, Tammy found she still couldn't make her legs move towards that door or Greg.

"Tammy?" Greg looked down at her with a warm smile. "I've been looking forward to–"

Their eyes met, and Greg's words froze in his throat at the icy stare she gave him. Tammy's eyes searched his, looking for the man she knew as Greg Watson, not this man in his expensively tailored suit and manicured hands. Her stomach lurched when she realized just how little she knew about Greg, and she was confused at how quickly he could change back into this persona. She'd only seen him that morning as the cowboy rancher.

"I'm sorry." Tammy shook her head, feeling sick to the stomach. "I thought I could do this, but I can't."

She turned to go, but he stopped her.

"Tammy, wait!" Greg called, and she could hear his heavy steps coming down the stairs.

She swung around. "Please, just leave me alone." Tammy stopped him from coming any further. "I think it best if you left Double A. I'll get Uncle Robert or Ashley to draw up an offer to buy your portion back from you."

"Tammy, can you please just hear me out?" Greg said in exasperation.

"No, I think I've heard and seen enough." Before he could say any more, Tammy spun around and started to walk towards the gate.

As she neared the entrance gate, the burner phone Jane had given her rang. Tammy fumbled in her pocket for it and answered.

"I've been calling you and calling you!" Jane hissed into the phone. "I have some important information for you."

"Where are you?" Tammy asked her.

"In my car heading toward you because I need you to come with me immediately," Jane told her.

"What's going on?" Tammy saw a car pull up, and Jane's head popped out the window as she beckoned her to the car.

Tammy ran to the car and got in the passenger seat. "Has something happened to Brynn?"

"No," Jane said, shaking her head. "But I have to get you to Holly's café."

"Why?" Tammy's heart was beating in her chest at the look on Jane's face.

"Once you left, I picked up a call on your normal phone," Jane glanced at her. "Sorry, we monitor everyone's phones that come to the locker."

"Is that what you call that underground hideout?" Tammy frowned.

"Yes." Jane nodded. "Anyway, a young girl named Christina phoned you, needing to see you urgently. She said she was at Holly's café."

"I don't know anyone named Christina." Tammy was confused.

"Well, she knows you. She and her brother need your help," Jane told her as she sped towards the center of Lewistown. They pulled to as top in front of Holly's cafe. "I called Holly to ask her to verify that there was a young girl and a young boy there, and she did."

"Okay?" Tammy got out of the car and was practically dragged into the café by Jane.

"That must be them!" Jane pointed to a table at the back of the café where a teenage girl sat with an elderly woman and a young dark-haired boy.

Tammy sucked in her breath. "That's Ursula's son, Marcus." She looked down at Jane, alarmed. "What are they doing here?"

"Guess we're going to find out." Jane quickly made her way to the table, leaving Tammy no option but to follow her.

"Miss. Anderson?" The young girl stood up and looked up at Tammy.

There was no hesitation in the girl's movements, even though Tammy picked up a flicker of doubt and fear that was gone in a flash. The girl was nervous but putting on a brave front.

"Yes," Tammy confirmed her identity. "I'm sorry, am I supposed to know who you are?" She looked at the young boy holding the elderly woman's hand. "Isn't that Marcus Guest?"

"Actually, he's Marcus Santiago, and I have all the proof for it." The young girl's chin raised defiantly.

"I believe you," Tammy's voice softened, and so did her features.

"Forgive my manners," Christina said. "I'm Christina Santiago. I think you knew my father, Carlos?"

"You're Carlos' daughter?" Tammy looked at her, shocked.

"Yes, and Marcus is my little brother." Christina turned. "This is my Nona, Estelle."

Estelle greeted Tammy with a warm smile.

"Why are you here, Christina?" Tammy asked her.

"Please, can you sit down?" Christina asked Tammy. She looked at Jane. "Thank you, Jane for helping us." She pointed to a chair for Jane.

"You're very welcome," Jane said, taking a chair as Tammy and Christina sat down.

"For the past eight years, we took care of Marcus under the guise of an au pair and a babysitter when my Nona got sick," Christina explained. "I go by my Nona's last name, Perez, as my pappa didn't want anyone to know about me. It is a long story, but the short version is he didn't want any of his Brazilian family finding out he was still alive or had children."

"My son-in-law was a good man, unlike his corrupt family," Estelle filled Tammy in. "He left everything behind, changed his face, and turned evidence against his family for my daughter's love."

"Yes, Nona, pappa was a good man and an incredible father," Christina confirmed. She turned to Tammy. "Ursula was engaged to my Pappa before she went off with your husband..." she stopped and looked at Tammy, "Forgive my rudeness."

"It's okay," Tammy assured her.

"Ursula was already pregnant then. My father found the test in the bathroom two weeks before she went off with Martin," Christina explained. "For five years, he hounded her for a paternity test, but she would not have one. A few months before pappa was killed, Marcus had to go to the hospital, and that was when my pappa got a court order for the test."

"Ursula didn't even bother to go to the hospital with Marcus," Estell said with disgust. "My Christina took him all on her own. That Ursula was never around. She used Marcus for photos with the press and to keep Martin Guest glued to her side."

"Should you be saying this in front of Marcus?" Tammy looked worriedly at the little boy who was busy playing on some hand-held device.

"He cannot hear. He has earphones," Christina assured Tammy. "When my father knew for sure Marcus was his, and I'd gotten evidence to show she was a neglectful mother, my papa took her to court, and they ordered my father get full custody." Her eyes started to mist over. "Ursula told the court she wanted to spend one last night with her son or, at least, keep him for the weekend while pappa went on that skiing business trip."

"The judge took pity on her and warned her that if Marcus was not handed to papa the day he arrived back, she would go to prison," Estelle continued the story. "Then my son-in-law got killed." Her eyes misted over with tears as well.

"Yesterday, Ursula got arrested as an accessory to multiple murders," Christina shocked Tammy and Jane by saying.

"Did you know about this?" Tammy looked at Jane, who shook her head.

"My papa wrote in his will, which he amended a few days before his ski trip, that you be Marcus' guardian." Christina pulled a copy of her father's will from the envelope. "Nona and I can no longer look after him by ourselves because her health is not good."

"Marcus has no one else," Estelle reached over and patted Tammy's hand. "We know you have been good to him even when you thought he was your husband's child."

"I..." Tammy swallowed, not sure what to say as her head was still reeling with the fact that Carlos Santiago, who hardly knew her, had left his son in her care. "What about you and your Nona?"

"We'll manage, somehow." Christina's chin once again lifted proudly. "My papa always told me that you never give up when you hit a speed bump. You keep going."

"Honey, that's so admirable of you," Tammy said as a thought took root. "Here's a crazy idea, though." She looked from Estelle to Christina. "I have a big ranch, and there is a wonderful school here, plus many care facilities for you to visit, Estelle."

"I do not want to live in a care facility!" Estelle's eyes narrowed.

"I would never suggest it," Tammy assured her. "I was suggesting that you all three come live with me. The care facilities were for you to go to for outings, make friends, and have any check-ups you may need."

"I..." Christina looked at Tammy in shocked amazement. "But you hardly know us!"

"I never knew your father that well," Tammy told her. "Yet he trusted me with his little boy, and I feel he knew I'd never let the three of you be separated."

"Maybe." Estelle looked thoughtful before looking at Christina and speaking to her in Spanish.

"We would like to accept your offer," Christina smiled and looked happily at her little brother. "On one condition."

"Let me guess," Tammy grinned. "Your Nona gets to do the cooking?" She teased.

"Something like that," Christina laughed. "No, she would like you to take over papa's business until either myself or Marcus is old enough to run it."

"We can talk about that as I know just the person who can help us with it." Tammy immediately thought about West and her Uncle Robert.

"Okay," Christina held out her hand. "It's a deal."

"Let's get you out to the ranch, and then we can chat about everything else," Tammy suggested.

"I'll drive you back to your car." Jane stood up.

Tammy walked side by side with the new additions to her ever growing family. There was a time when she thought she'd never get to be a mother and now here she was with three children to be a mother figure for. Four if you counted Greg's daughter but after today, Tammy was sure they wouldn't be at Double A ranch for much longer.

"Oh, Tammy, there's something you should know about Greg!" Jane said before sliding into her car.

"Okay," Tammy slid into the passenger seat once Christina, Estelle, and Marcus were safely in the back.

"Well..." The next words out of Jane's mouth had Tammy struck dumb with shock.

# Chapter Four

# MEANT FOR EACH OTHER

Greg ran to the house's front door and saw his brother standing and staring at the complex's gate.

"Bronwyn told me that Tammy was here," Greg said to him.

"Uh…" Grayson-Wyatt Watson looked at his younger brother. "She was!" He pulled a face.

"What did you do?" Greg's eyes narrowed, and he felt his heart squeeze in his chest.

"I think she thought I was you!" Grayson looked at his brother apologetically. "She told me to pack up my things and leave the Double A."

"Please tell me you put her straight?" Greg looked up at the sky and clenched his fists at his side.

"I tried!" Grayson put his hands up apologetically. "She rushed out here, a car picked her up, and then went squealing off at a heck of speed before I could get to it."

"What car?" Greg's face paled, and he felt his heart drop.

"I don't know, some pink girly Mini type of car!" Grayson grimaced.

"Oh, that would be Jane's car," Ashley's voice made Greg spin around. "I'll call her and see where they went." She pulled her phone out of her pocket and rang Jane, who answered after a few short rings.

Greg stood impatiently waiting as Ashley uh-huhed what felt like a few thousand times.

"Well?" Greg hissed.

"You've still got it bad for Tammy, don't you, little brother?" Grayson teased Greg.

"I'm warning you, Watts!" Greg glared at his brother. "This time, I won't take the fall for your mess."

"Oh, come now," Grayson said defensively. "That wasn't my mess, buddy. If you weren't such a stubborn hothead, you'd have stormed after her and made her listen to you."

"I was trying to save your future wife and her mother from that abusive father of hers," Greg reminded him, "While you were throwing a party at our house."

"I was literally a few doors away, and you should've come straight to me." Greyson's posture changed as his eyes narrowed dangerously. "You nearly got yourself killed twice that night."

"Thanks to you!" Greg raised his voice angrily.

"You were passed out from that blow to your head!" Grayson held his ground. "We were trying to rush you and Bron to the hospital. She got knifed while trying to create a diversion from you and her mother, if you remember."

"Okay, you two can zip it!" Ashley's voice cracked like a whip between them, and they both stopped to glare at her. "Jane said that Tammy's on her way home to Double A."

Greg stood looking at Ashley for a few minutes, not knowing what to do. He wanted to rush off after Tammy and explain everything, but his legs wouldn't move.

"Oh boy!" Grayson rolled his eyes, pulled out his phone, and called his driver. "I need you to take my brother to the Double A ranch."

"Are you going to stand there gaping at me like a goldfish?" Ashley asked him. "Or are you finally going to put that pride of yours in your pocket and make things right with Tammy?"

"I bet he messes it up!" Grayson grinned, knowing he was baiting his brother.

"That's a horrible thing to say to your brother!" Bronwyn walked towards them, stopping in front of Greg. "Greg, you can do this. We all know how deeply in love with Tammy you are and have always been. Now's your chance to go and make things right." She raised an eyebrow. "Because if I haven't heard back that you and she have finally talked this out, I'll go speak to her myself."

That snapped Greg out of his frozen state as the limo pulled up to take him to Double A.

"I'm going!"

Tammy had just got her new housemates settled when she heard a car pull up outside. She turned to tell Molly she'd get the door, and to her surprise, the room was deserted. Estelle and Molly, who had been sitting in there, chatting, had disappeared. Tammy frowned and looked around for the four children who'd had also mysteriously vanished. The house was suddenly empty, and Tammy felt like she'd stepped into some alternate dimension as a strange silence settled over her home.

Before she could think more about where everyone had gone, she heard heavy footsteps coming up the stairs and went to get the door. Except before she got there, it flew open, and as it did, she caught a glimpse of the eight people who lived with her piling into a limo outside.

"I guess we're here all alone?" Greg's voice startled her as she suddenly realized it was him who'd walked through the door.

She'd been so surprised to see the door swing open and everyone pile into the limo that she hadn't noticed him standing there.

"It seems so!" Tammy swallowed, and her heart started hammering in her chest. "Whose limo is that?"

"Someone I'm going to strangle later!" Greg said, his eyes locking with Tammy.

They stood staring at each in front of the open door, neither of them knowing what to say.

"Tammy," Greg started at the same time Tammy said, "Greg I..."

They both laughed, and, before they knew it, their lips crushed against each other. Tammy's hands snaked around the back of Greg's neck while his strong arms pulled her to him. A bark made them jump apart as three bassets barreled towards them. They danced around their feet for a few seconds before they trotted off into the living room and sat in front of the fire.

"I need to say something!" Greg was the first to break the silence.

"I do, too," Tammy said. "But you go first."

"Tammy, Bronwyn, and I were never really a couple. She was in love with someone else, and we just pretended to be together when I was in high school." Greg ran his hands through his hair. "It was a stupid deal she and I made. I hated girls trying to get me to go out with them. There was only one girl I ever wanted to go out with, and she was unavailable to me. While Bronwyn didn't want to look like she didn't have a boyfriend and didn't want to seem like she was making hers up because he lived and went to school in Billings."

"Okay..." Tammy looked up at him.

"That night at the prom, she came to me to ask me to help her and her mother," Greg told Tammy. "They were planning on running away from her father that night, but he'd caught her mother trying to sneak out and had caused a scene."

"I didn't know," Tammy's voice dropped and her heart went out to Bronwyn and her mother.

"When we realized you were there, I was still angry about her father and then even more so when I saw the look in your eyes." He looked down at the ground. "When you refused to hear me out, I was hurt and angry when I realized what you must've thought. I couldn't believe that you would think so little of me that I would be using you to get back with Bronwyn."

"Greg..." Tammy started to say, but he cut her off and took her hands.

"Tammy, I was an idiot, and I should've forced you to listen to me." Greg pulled her hands against his chest. "Maybe if I had, we never would've spent the last thirty-seven years apart, but together where we belong."

"I..." Tammy started, but he put his finger over her lips.

"You said I could go first." Greg smiled teasingly down at her, and she nodded. "Tammy, I am so hopelessly in love with you. I have always been and always will be. Even my daughter and Brynn picked up on it and told me to stop being an idiot and tell you."

"Wise girls, those two," Tammy said with a smile.

"I know," Greg agreed with her.

"Can I speak now?" Tammy asked him.

"No, I have something else to tell you." Gregg gave her a quick kiss. "The man Bronwyn is in love with, married to, and had children with is..."

"I know. He's your older brother," Tammy finished for him.

"Not that much older," Greg put the record straight. "Only forty-five minutes, in fact."

"Your twin!" Tammy realized. "Of course, he is. That's why you look almost identical."

"I'm glad you said almost because I, for one, have always thought I was the better-looking one." Greg gave her a cheeky grin. "Okay, now it's your turn."

Tammy gently untangled herself from his embrace. "Thank you for telling me what you did. All I wanted to say was that I know that Grayson Wyatt is your brother and that his name is really Grayson Wyatt Watson. Known as Watts to his friends and family. And that he was the one who'd been driving the car the night of the accident."

Tammy stepped back from Greg. Her heart felt like it had been magically healed, with all the pieces fitting perfectly back into place. Greg grabbed her hand and pulled her back towards him for another heart-stopping kiss. When he lifted his head, he looked deep into her eyes. "I love you, Tammy, and want to spend the rest of my life with you."

"I'm sorry, Greg, for jumping to conclusions all those years ago and then again this afternoon," Tammy admitted. "I don't really want you to leave Double A."

"Oh yes, I believe you asked Grayson to pack his bags and leave Double A." Greg laughed.

"I feel like such an idiot. How am I going to face him ever again?" Tammy felt her cheeks heat up as she looked up into Greg's green-gold eyes.

"Don't worry about it. Grayson has a whacky sense of humor and thoroughly enjoyed being told off as me," Greg assured her. "I think you're his favorite person right now."

"Oh, I see, sibling rivalry!" Tammy laughed. "I miss that." She felt her eyes mist over as thoughts of Brian flashed through her mind. "Do you think this is what Brian intended when he set you up here?"

"I like to think so," Greg told her. "He knew I was madly in love with you."

"He knew I was madly in love with you as well." Tammy finally admitted her feeling for Greg out loud, and she felt her heart soar while their souls reached out to each other. "I love you, Greg, and want to spend the rest of my life with you."

"Can we get married tomorrow?" Greg asked her, grinning.

"I want to say yes, but we need a license, and I think we'll get a blistering from our family and our friends if we do that," Tammy warned him.

"I guess you're right." Greg sighed and kissed her again. "Do you think we can move into the living room and curl up in front of the fire next to the bassets?"

"Yes, I think that's a brilliant idea." Tammy took his hand while he kicked the door closed and led him into the living room.

Once they'd made themselves comfortable on a few soft

cushions on the floor, Greg put his arm around her and pulled her close to his side.

"Speaking of family," Greg said, looking down at her. "Did I notice we had three more people than usual?"

"Oh, yes!" Tammy looked up at him. "How do you feel about being a father to two more children and an honorary son to Nona Estelle?"

"Are you going to tell me who I'll be agreeing to adopt?" Greg looked down at her questioningly.

"Of course, but it's quite a long story, and I'm starving." Tammy grinned back up at him.

"Well, let's go see what's in the kitchen, and then you can tell me all about it over dinner with some wine." Greg pulled her up and kissed her once more.

"Deal!" Tammy agreed as they walked hand in hand towards the kitchen. "I still have many questions about that prom night," she told him as they looked for something to eat.

"I know," Greg nodded. "But can we put that on hold for tonight?" He looked into her eyes. "I just want to enjoy us finally being able to tell each other how we feel. I want tonight to be only about you and me."

"I can agree to that!" Tammy's voice grew hoarse with emotion as she kissed his cheek. "Oh, there are actually four more people as Nona has a new housekeeper for us."

"I'm sure your parents, Greg, and Lynn, are delighted that this big old house will be filled with love, laughter, and children again." Greg pulled her to him, and their lips met in a dance of love as the world around them faded away.

# Chapter Five

# SAVING AMY - PART 1

Amy loved soaring across the wide-open space of the Montana countryside, breathing in the fresh air. Pegasus, a nineteen-hand high sorrel Percheron with a golden main and tail, was on loan to her from the Cupids Bow stables. When Amy first saw Pegasus, she's fallen in love with the four-year-old, who had the most awesome nature. Cat's niece, who owned Pegasus, said she was sure the horse felt the same way about Amy. The two had bonded on sight.

"At least someone loves me!" Amy said to the wind as she and Pegasus flew across the land.

She didn't have a destination in mind. All Amy needed to do was get out of the house for a couple of hours. While she appreciated Tammy taking her in and looking after her, Amy was all better now and needed to start straightening out her own life. She knew where she needed to start, and that was a look into how she had landed at a rehab facility. Amy didn't do drugs. She very rarely took an aspirin. Amy preferred alternative treatments like acupuncture, acupressure, hot rocks, and herbal teas. Yet she had landed in an institute to get clean like her brother and the rest of the world had told her.

Amy knew she should be mourning her brother, but she was still too angry at him. Martin wouldn't believe her when she told him she was being drugged. Instead, Martin had accused her of being just like their father and becoming too addicted to pain medication and alcohol. Amy had hardly touched pain medication. Heck, she was so paranoid about drug and alcohol abuse that she insisted every one of her sets, cast members, and crew were tested. Amy refused to work with anyone under the influence of a mind-altering substance. She never drank alcohol except for an occasional sip for a toast.

Everyone who knew Amy knew she was anti-drugs and against alcohol. She was like that because she knew first-hand how it could endanger other people's lives. Amy had been in the car the night her father had died when he'd flipped it because he'd been under the influence of pain meds he'd washed down with bourbon. She had also nearly died and was in critical condition when they rushed her into the hospital.

Amy still had burn marks on her back, and it had taken years of painful skin grafts to get them to look like what they did today. She still had a slight limp whenever her hip, which had been fractured in the accident, slipped out. That happened more often, especially as she got older. Amy was only thirteen at the time of the accident. Martin should've known she was telling the truth when she insisted someone was drugging her. Amy had never gotten a prescription for the painkiller they had told her she allegedly abused after her back injury. She didn't even know who the doctor on the prescription Martin had found in her purse was. But the more Amy had denied it, the guiltier she looked.

*You more than anyone should know, Amy, that addicts lie!* Amy could still hear her brother's voice dripping with disappointment and disdain. *I remember dad telling mom that he hadn't taken anything when he was clearly lying. I cannot sit here and watch you go down the same slippery slope dad did.*

Tears stung Amy's eyes as she remembered being marched into the facility. The endless hours of therapy. At first, she'd tried to tell the doctors that she was being drugged and someone was trying to get rid of her. But they wouldn't listen. They would only tell her that is what the drugs did to her; they made her delusional and paranoid. Eventually, Amy just gave up trying to fight and stopped trying to tell them she wasn't an addict. But they were right about one thing. That ordeal had made her paranoid. For the first time in her life, she could understand why kings or queens of the old years had food testers. Amy knew it was a bit overkill to hire a food tester, and that would make her look batty.

But she had made up her mind that once she got out of that horrid place, she would be more careful with her food and beverages. She would not let just anyone serve her food or anything to drink. Amy would be darned if she'd ever get into this situation again. How did her life just get taken over by someone who had stolen her voice and control? It was frightening just how easy it was to be accused of doing something. Then when you tried to convey your innocence, no one listened because the more you protested, the guiltier you looked. The sad thing was that once you were accused of being an addict, people only saw you that way; no one stopped to think that it wasn't true.

It was easier to believe a lie than to swallow an ugly truth, especially when that truth may involve having to go up against a Guest. Even when her brother, Martin's, affair hit the news, the world was only shocked for a few seconds before forgiving the golden boy of talk shows. When he got fired from the network their family owned, Martin came out of it smelling like roses as he announced his leaving for early retirement. Amy knew the truth about why Martin got fired, and she'd toyed with the idea of leaking that bit of information to the press as her revenge. But Amy didn't work that way. Revenge was nothing more than a vicious circle of 'hit me, and I hit you back.' In the end, it was just exhausting and could consume a person when there was so much else to be spending your time doing.

Like getting to the bottom of who had been drugging her. Amy had landed a big part in a movie when word of how well she'd done at the wellness center started circulating. She knew it was thanks to Tammy, who was silently cleaning up her reputation, and it was her way of telling Amy she believed her story. Amy was so glad when Tammy had finally come to her senses and seen Martin for what he really was and had always been. Her brother was a womanizer. Amy loved her big brother, but that didn't mean she liked him. They had never really gotten along, and the only reason she visited them as often as she did was that Amy and Tammy had become best friends. She was the sister Amy had always wished she had in her dream family.

Instead, Amy had been raised by au pairs and dressed up as the perfect little princess daughter for family photoshoots to portray her mother as the perfect single parent celebrity. She'd never meant to get into acting; she had just fallen into it. If she was being honest with herself, the past year spent without an acting job had been like an extended vacation for her. Amy was thinking of giving up acting, and she would have, had she not been almost broke thanks to her brother. Once again, a spurt of anger flashed through her at the thought of her brother, and she felt guilty about it.

Amy slowed Pegasus down to a walk as they came across a river. She walked him along its banks for a while before coming across a bridge. Amy slid off the horse and walked him over to it.

"Are you okay to cross it, boy?" Amy reached up and rubbed Pegasus' head.

Carefully, she started to lead him over the bridge, but as they got to the other side, the large horse jolted and shook his great head as he slightly reared up, knocking Amy backward. Her arms flew over her head as her body fell towards the river. Amy tried to step back to regain her balance, but she twisted her ankle, landing in a heap with her bottom on the wet, muddy riverbank. Before she got up, she noted Pegasus was lifting his front hoof from the ground.

"Oh no, boy!" Amy said worriedly.

Amy tried to stand up, but a hot searing pain sliced through her ankle, making her legs buckle. This time, before she hit the mud, a pair of strong arms reached out and grabbed her.

"Watch it!" A deep voice tickled her ear. "Are you okay?"

Amy looked up into two hazel eyes surrounded by thick lashes and set in a handsome face scowling at her.

"I'm fine," Amy lied, trying to pull herself out of his arms, only to nearly topple over again.

"You don't look fine!" His voice was clipped. "Let me take a look at that ankle."

"I'm fine. It's my horse that needs looking at!" Amy insisted. "I think there is something wrong with his hoof." She frowned at him. "You're Ryan?"

"I am." He nodded, ignoring her request to look at her horse as he helped her over to the bridge and sat her down to examine her ankle. "It doesn't seem to be broken, but it's defiantly sprained."

"That's just great as that's my good leg!" Amy grumbled.

"I beg your pardon?" Ryan frowned at her.

"Nothing!" Amy didn't feel like getting into her skiing accident and her broken leg or weird hip. *Goodness, I sound like an old crock*, she mused. "Could you please look at my horse's hoof?"

"I can see he is not happy," Ryan turned to look at Pegasus. "Why are you riding a horse like Pegasus?" He looked at her with narrowed eyes. "Cat's daughter should've given you a more suitable horse."

Amy couldn't believe what he'd just said to her, and she sat there staring at him in disbelief. Ryan spoke gently to Pegasus and stroked his neck while the horse gently blew and nudged him. The horse obviously knew the rude man.

"I'm going to look at your hoof. Okay, boy?" Ryan gave the long shiny neck one more pat before skillfully lifting Pegasus' hoof. "He has a large stone wedged in his hoof."

"Oh no." Amy's voice filled with worry. "Can you get it out?"

"Yes," Ryan told her, his voice flickering with anger. "Didn't you notice he was limping?" He looked at Pegasus. "I felt his skin was wet with perspiration, so you were obviously riding him fast."

"We were having a bit of a gallop." Amy's hackles were rising.

She didn't like Ryan's accusing tone and the looks of anger he kept throwing her way.

"Pegasus is a big powerful horse," Ryan got a weird-looking tweezer-type tool from one of his saddlebags and walked back to Pegasus. "He needs to be ridden with care. He is also still a young horse that is barely old enough to ride."

Ryan lifted Pegasus' hoof and gently removed the stone. Amy watched how gentle and patient he was with the horse while he had given her a tongue lashing without knowing anything about her horse skills. She took offense, and anger started to boil inside her.

"I know all about Pegasus." Amy's voice was low and held a hint of her boiling temper.

She was already a good three heads or so shorter than Ryan's six-foot-three height. Well, at least to her five-foot-five, he looked that tall. Amy felt even smaller seated on the bridge, so she awkwardly pulled herself up, leaning against the rail for support. She ignored the pain throbbing through her ankle.

"You should be sitting with that ankle up." Ryan glanced at her and then back at Pegasus hoof as he tested it for bruising.

"Sure," Amy said sarcastically. "I'll just recline right here on my easy chair."

Ryan lifted his head, and his eyes narrowed as he looked at her, "Luckily, his hoof doesn't seem to have any bruising."

"That's because he only stepped on the stone when he came off the bridge," Amy told him smugly. "Which I walked him over before you go telling me off about how to cross a bridge with a horse!"

Ryan let Pegasus hoof go and gently lowered it to the ground before standing up. "There you go, boy!" He patted the horse, put a hand into his vest pocket, and pulled out a bag of carrots and cut apple pieces. He took a few pieces from it. "Here you go."

Pegasus loved that and chomped the fruit from Ryan's hand. Ryan turned back towards her. "I'm sorry." He took Amy by surprise by apologizing to her. "It was wrong of me to attack you like that."

"Oh!" Amy was at a loss for words and didn't quite know what to say. "I grew up around horses and have ridden my entire life, you know."

"I should've asked before jumping to conclusions about a city slicker," Ryan said, throwing in a barb.

"So, cowboys really use that term?" Amy shook her head.

"What term?" Ryan frowned.

"City slicker, an idiomatic derogatory term for us urbanites who country folk think have no business traipsing around in the country." Amy would've folded her arms across her chest, but she had to hang onto the bridge post, so she raised her eyebrows instead.

"No," Ryan said, shaking his head. "We have a much more derogatory term for that." He put the tweezer tool back into his saddlebags and closed it before turning back to her. "But as you're an actress, I thought it might be fitting."

"Oh, so you do know who I am?" Amy nodded.

"Even if I didn't," Ryan walked to Pegasus and checked the hoof one last time before standing up and dusting off his hands. "The entire countryside is buzzing with news of you being here, and my niece has been babbling on about it since you arrived."

"Great!" Amy closed her eyes and shook her head. "Now the whole world knows where I've gone to lick my wounds, and they probably think I'm off drying out again." She muttered beneath her breath.

"Excuse me?" Ryan looked at her.

"Nothing!" Amy's eyes shot open and collided with Ryan's hazel ones.

A strange look passed through his eyes before his features softened, and he looked pointedly at her ankle.

"We need to get you off that foot and get it iced." Ryan's voice and demeanor softened. "It will have to hang down for a few minutes when I ride you back to my ranch."

"It's okay," Amy said, suddenly panicked about putting him out. "I can ride back to Double A."

"No, you can't," Ryan told her.

Before she could stop him, Ryan was upon her, scooping her up as if she was as light as a feather. She had no option but to link her arms around his neck to balance them. When she did that, their eyes locked and held as they stared at each for a few seconds. Electricity shot through Amy like her heart had slid across a carpet and then touched a metal object − a feeling she had felt in a long time fluttered in her belly. Pegasus stomped on the ground, breaking the spell as Ryan stiffened and his head shot around. Amy followed his gaze and froze when she saw what looked like a flash from a camera in the distance.

"Oh no!" Amy hissed and instinctively buried her head in his chest as she tried to hide her face. "Reporters!"

Ryan's body stiffened, and his arms tightened around her just a bit, "Don't worry about it. Hang on. I'll lift you onto Daisy's back."

Amy's eyes flew open, and she looked up at the tall ruggedly handsome cowboy. He was all macho man, complete with a broody nature, and he rode a horse named Daisy! Amy had to bite her lip to stop herself from bursting into laughter, but the bubbling laughter soon died when he plonked her on his horse.

"Sorry," Ryan said, "You're a lot lighter than I anticipated."

"Gee, thanks," Amy said, feeling slightly deflated by his comment after their smoldering eye contact.

Or at least it felt smoldering to her. She quickly shook away her romantic thoughts. Amy had always been a bit of a romantic, and she secretly loved reading romances or acting in romantic movies. The way Ryan had saved her may have been a bit rocky, but it was like a classic beginning of a love story.

*Stop it, Amy!* She admonished her wayward thoughts. Besides, from what she'd heard about Ryan Beckett, there was not a single romantic bone in his body.

"I really can ride back to Double A," Amy insisted.

"No, you cannot," Ryan said again, securing Pegasus' reins

before swinging up on his beautiful blue roan quarter horse. "You need to get that ankle up on ice, and my ranch is the closest." He tilted his head towards where they'd seen the flash. "You also don't want to go back towards Double A because we seem to have watchers."

"Watchers?" Amy asked, her head shooting towards the side the flash had come from.

"Yup," Ryan spurred his horse into a gallop, with Pegasus following suit as Ryan skillfully handled both horses. "Are you okay back there?"

Ryan turned as Amy's arms shot around his waist when he took off, and she nearly toppled backward. As she righted herself and lessened her grip on his waist, another flash of light caught her eyes.

"That's just great!" Amy muttered again. "I'm fine!" She said a little louder so he could hear her. "But it seems we've had another picture taken of us."

"Well, let's hope it is the paparazzi!" Ryan glanced back towards where the flash had come from.

"Why?" Amy asked him, surprised, having to raise her voice as the wind filled her mouth.

"Because it's the better alternative to someone stalking you who is involved in all the trouble around here." He glanced down at her foot. "Is your foot okay?"

Amy was once again surprised by the genuine concern she heard in his voice. "It's just throbbing a little. Nothing I can't handle."

"We're nearly there," Ryan promised as they rode into a thicket of trees.

Ryan slowed Daisy and Pegasus down as he navigated them carefully through the trees, careful not to get Pegasus' reins caught up. Once they cleared the trees, Amy's eyes widened as she took in the beautiful old three-story ranch house with a wraparound veranda. Large stone chimneys stood on either side of the house. Two log cabins were on each side, joined by a roof with a dogtrot in the middle. Three large windmills stood off to one side next to the cabins, and an older style windmill that looked like it had been well taken care of stood a few feet away from the farthest log cabin with a well in front of it.

"This is beautiful," Amy told Ryan as they led the horses around to the back of the house.

The scenery at the back of the house took Amy's breath away. The back garden sloped down for a few meters. There was a large stable off to the one side and paddocks next to the barns. A clear well-kept grassy lawn stretched between the two sides, making a clear path down to the sparkling banks of a river. The Snowy Mountains loomed in the distance as if guarding the peaceful scene in front of her.

"Oh wow!" Amy breathed, taking in the beauty of her surroundings. "That river is amazing. This entire property is beautiful. You have a bit of everything." Her head turned. "You are surrounded by woods, water, and mountains."

"Yes, I think we got the best deal out of all the ranches," Ryan said proudly. "There are four rivers that run through our property. All branching from that one." He inclined his head towards the river at the bottom of the property. "That forms part of Bow River."

"It's beautiful." Amy had to put her hands on his shoulders for support as he took her down from Daisy's back.

Their eyes met and held as he gently lowered her to the ground, but the spell was once again broken – this time, by an excited feminine voice. Ryan stepped back and released her so quickly that she almost topped backward. He reached out to steady her, and she smiled gratefully at him before turning her attention to the back door of the ranch house.

"Uncle Ryan!" Avery Beckett bolted out of the back door of the ranch house. "Have you brought me an early birthday gift?"

She stopped and gave Avery a wide smile. Amy knew in that instant that the woman was a fan, and it felt good to see one of her fans still look at her in adoration instead of disgust.

# Chapter Six

# SAVING AMY - PART 2

The beautiful young woman walked towards them. Her long black hair was tied in a braid and hung over her one shoulder. She wore faded blue jeans with a light orange and yellow striped cotton snap shirt, and her bootleg jeans allowed the tips of well-worn boots to peak out. Just like all the other ranchers, her jeans were cinched at the waist by a leather belt with a buckle that was not as big as Ryan's was. Amy had starred in a Western and had to learn about ranch clothing.

They wore cotton shirts with snaps in case they got tangled up, and their shirt was easy to pull off. The same went for the buckles on their belts. If the belt got caught, it would pop open so the rancher could free themselves.

"Hi!" Amy's cheeks flamed at being caught sharing another smoldering look with the broody Ryan Beckett. "I'm..."

"Amy Guest," Avery smiled, and dimples dented her creamy cheeks that were spattered with dusty pink freckles. Her brown eyes sparkled with excitement and warmth as she looked at Amy. "I'm Avery, Ryan's favorite niece."

"My only niece is what she meant to say," Ryan corrected. "Avery, do you mind gawking at our guest inside?" He laughed at the glare she shot him. "Miss Guest has sprained her ankle and needs to put it on ice."

"It's Amy," Amy corrected Ryan. "And I'm sure I can hobble there myself."

"Avery looked down at Amy's ankle and then back up at her. "I really don't think you should try," she advised Amy. "It looks like a rather nasty sprain to me. In fact, I think I may need you to have an X-ray."

"Are you a doctor?" Amy looked at her, surprised.

"I'm doing my residency right now at the local hospital in Lewistown," Avery told her. "Uncle Ryan, I think you need to carry Amy into the living room if you can." She grinned at Amy's widening eyes. "You can sit in the new recliner." She winked teasingly.

"That's my chair!" Ryan glared at Avery, and before Amy could protest, he once again swooped her off her feet and into his strong arms.

Amy's heart instantly kicked into double-time, quickening her pulse and making that weird flutter in her belly happen again. She tried as hard as she could to control her beating heart and concentrated on the décor inside the house. There were a lot of antiques that were well mixed in with more modern pieces of furniture. The kitchen, from what she could see while Ryan rushed her through it, was large and had been modernized to a country style.

"The house is decorated like it should be appearing in a country home magazine." Amy's eyes darted around the living room as Ryan put her down on a black leather chair.

Amy nearly screamed in fright when Ryan flicked a button on the side of the chair, and things sprung back while a leg rest shot out.

"Sorry," Ryan said apologetically. "But our resident doctor here insists your ankle gets elevated."

"I did," Avery admitted walking into the room as Ryan straightened up. "I have an ice pack for your ankle." She knelt in front of the chair. "Do you mind if I examine your ankle properly?" She looked at Avery, who shook her head. "I'm going to need to take your sneaker off."

"Okay." Amy started to lean forward to do it, but Avery stopped her. "You relax. Uncle Ryan will get you some peppermint tea and an herbal salve I make myself for the pain."

"Thank you," Amy smiled at Avery. "I appreciate that."

"No problem," Avery told her. Her look told Amy that she completely understood and knew a lot about Amy.

Ryan walked back into the living room, surprising Amy, who'd been so caught up talking to Avery that she hadn't realized he had left. He was carrying a tray with a teapot and a cup on it.

"Here is your peppermint tea." Ryan placed the tray on the side table next to Amy. "This is the salve you asked me to get." He handed Avery a bottle with a green paste in it.

Avery took it from him. "I'll put some of this on after the ice pack has been on for a while."

"Avery, have you seen where my glasses are?" A woman who looked like an older version of Avery with a neat shoulder-length bob stepped into the living and stopped dead when she saw Amy. "My goodness, Amy, what happened to you?"

"Hi, Gwen," Amy smiled up at the woman she'd met the other day while in Lewistown with her sister-in-law, Tammy. "I had a bit of an incident while out riding. Your brother saved me and brought me back here."

"And rightly so." Gwen walked into the room. "I hope you're taking good care of our guest, Avery?"

"No, mom, I was about to ask Uncle Ryan to get the saw so we could chop off her foot!" Avery raised her eyebrows as she looked at her mother.

"I knew you'd somehow manage to rub off on her!" Gwen glared at her younger brother before turning back to her daughter. "You know what I think about sarcasm, dear."

"Mommy, I think you only feel that way because you have no sense of humor!" Avery and Ryan's fists bumped at that revelation.

"Why don't you two go and get me a cup of tea while I sit here catching up with Amy!" It was more of an order than a request from Gwen, who was clearly the queen of the house.

"Right!" Ryan said, spinning on his heel and leaving the room with his niece right behind him.

"Forgive them," Gwen rolled her eyes. "Can you imagine my mortification when my beautiful baby girl turned out to be a replica of my younger brother?"

"She seems to have turned out to be a lovely young woman." Amy smiled at Gwen. "And she's a doctor."

"Yes, I am very proud of hers and my brothers' accomplishments." Gwen looked at Amy. Sadness flitted through her eyes. "Sadly, they've both had such hard knocks in their life that I fear it has hardened their hearts and locked away their beautiful souls."

"I'm sorry to hear that." Amy watched as Gwen walked over to the table next to the chair where Amy was sitting.

"May I pour you some of your tea?" Gwen asked.

"I can do it," Amy said, not wanting to be any more of a bother than she was already feeling.

"It's okay. You need to keep that foot the way my daughter left it." Gwen laughed. "She takes her patients' healing very seriously."

Gwen poured Amy a steaming cup of tea and poured some honey into it, telling Amy that it came from Avery and Ryan's beehives.

"Really?" Amy was impressed. "It tastes amazing," she said after a sip of her tea."

"Yes, we all expected Avery to become a vet. She loves wildlife," Gwen told her. "It was surprising when she announced after a year of working in a vet's office when she finished school, she wanted to be a doctor."

"Did she not like working with animals in a vet capacity?" Amy took another sip of the delicious tea. "This peppermint tea is amazing."

"Thank you," Gwen grinned. "I made it. It is one of the herbal teas my company makes."

"That's right." Amy looked into the cup. "Tammy told me you own Gwen's Natural Supplements and Foods."

"Yes," Gwen confirmed. "We also now have a line of one-hundred percent natural, cruelty-free cosmetics. My team is working on a perfume."

"That's incredible." Amy looked around the living room. "I love the décor in your house."

"That was my former company." Gwen laughed when she saw the look on Amy's face. "My late husband, Reece Manfred, and I started it together. When he passed away, I put my everything into making our dream into the reality that it became."

"No!" Amy's eyes widened as she realized who Gwen was. "Manfred's Creation was yours?"

"It was!" Gwen, who was sitting on a sofa next to Amy, looked around the room. "We used the ranch house to photograph our pieces."

"I loved your pieces." Amy took another sip of her tea before putting her cup on the table. "I have..." She stopped as she remembered her brother had forced her to sell her properties and possessions. "Or rather, I had a lot of your pieces."

"Wow." Gwen looked at Amy in surprise. "Amy Guest had some of our furniture in her house. I'm flattered."

"Oh no, I'm in awe," Amy admitted. "Tammy knows how much I love natural products and only ever take herbal alternatives to real medication." She waited for the usual look of disbelief in Gwen's eyes when she said that, but there was none. "When she introduced me to your products and told me it was from someone from her hometown, I was amazed."

"Once again, I'm flattered," Gwen said. "I can give you some samples of our cosmetic and skincare range if you want to try them."

"I would love that!" Amy's eyes lit up. "But not free samples. I will buy them."

"I won't take your money, Amy," Gwen told her. "Please do not take that as an insult. It is not intended as one. I know there's been anger and rift in the ranches surrounding ours. But we are family at the end of the day. As the other ranches know, I don't accept money when looking after my family's well-being."

"That is very kind of you." Amy felt humbled by the beautiful woman with her warm, compassionate brown eyes smiling at her.

"Ah, it's about time." Gwen looked up as Avery walked in with another tea tray which had some sandwiches on it as well.

"It took so long because I was making you something to eat, and Uncle Ryan kept eating the sandwiches as soon as they were done!" Avery shook her head frustratedly.

"He always could eat like a horse." Gwen sighed. "My older brother and I raised Ryan after my father passed away."

"My gran left my mom, my late Uncle Todd, and Uncle Ryan when he was only five," Avery explained, stopping Amy from asking about their mother. "She ran off with a ranch hand."

"Oh, I'm sorry," Amy said, looking at Gwen. "I know what it's like to lose a parent at a crucial age."

"That was your father, right?" Avery blurted out before her mother could stop her.

"Avery!" Gwen breathed, looking at her daughter with a stern expression. "That was rather callous of you."

"I'm sorry." Avery pulled a face, picking up the sandwiches and offering one to Amy.

"Thank you. I'm starving," Amy admitted taking two, not caring if they thought badly of her.

She actually wanted to take more but didn't want them to compare her to Ryan.

"Here you go." Avery handed her plate. "Are you sure you don't want to take a few more?" she glanced at the door. "If my uncle walks back in here, there will be none left."

"Don't mind if I do!" Amy thought, what the heck, and took two more. They were cut into triangles, so four of them only really added up to a sandwich, she reasoned.

"I told you not to cut them into triangles." Ryan's voice at the door made Amy's heart jump, and her sandwich-holding hand froze mid-air to her mouth. "I'll make sure Pegasus is rubbed down correctly before getting him ready to ride back to Double A."

"Oh, are you keeping Pegasus at Double A?" Avery looked questioningly at Amy.

"Yes. Jamie, Cat's niece, has loaned him to me while I here," Amy explained. She looked at Ryan. "But I'll ride him as soon as I've rested my ankle enough."

"You most certainly will not!" Avery poured tea for her mother and then herself before sitting on the sofa next to Gwen. "As your new doctor, while you're in Montana, I forbid you to ride for at least a week. One of us will drive you back to the Double A tomorrow."

"Tomorrow?" Ryan and Amy said together, both looking at Avery.

"Yes, I don't want you moving around with that ankle until it's been rested for a good twenty-four hours." Avery grinned smugly up at her uncle.

"I'll take Pegasus back to Double A and inform Tammy about what happened," Ryan addressed Amy.

"I can phone…" Amy remembered she didn't have her phone. "Oh, shoot I forgot my phone at Double A."

"It's really irresponsible of you to go off riding on your own in the countryside you're not familiar with without your phone." Ryan's eyes narrowed on her. "Especially with all the trouble that has been happening around here."

"And where is your phone, Ryan?" Gwen looked up at her brother with raised brows.

"I…" Ryan patted his pockets. "I left it in the kitchen."

"Sure, you did, Uncle Ryan." Avery gave him another cheeky grin, not fazed by his black look.

"Can I have a word with you?" Ryan glared at his niece.

"Do I need my mother to be with me?" Avery took a sip of her tea.

"I just need your help with Pegasus, if you must know!" Ryan sighed. "He got a stone in his hoof, and I just want to make sure he's okay."

"You could've just said that!" Avery rolled her eyes. "Instead,

you make me think you want to chop my head off about
something."

"I did not," Ryan defended himself, shaking his head. "Now,
will you please come help me so I can get the horse back before
nightfall?"

"I'll come fetch you in your new pickup from Double A!"
Avery suggested.

"Well played!" Ryan raised an eyebrow at his niece. "You can
drive it this once, but remember one scratch on it..."

Amy watched the comradery between uncle and niece. She
could feel the love and how close the family was. It was the type
of family Amy had wished she'd been blessed with. Instead, she
got two parents who she knew loved her. But they loved their
celebrity status and high-profile careers more. To them, Amy
had just been a prop they loved to make the world see them as
this perfect power couple, but a prop, nonetheless.

"I know, I know!" Avery finished her tea and then followed
Ryan out of the lounge, stopping at the living room door. "We'll
see you at dinner. Can I ask Aunt Tammy to get you a change of
clothing when I'm there?"

"Yes, please," Amy hadn't thought about a change of clothes.
"She'll know what to get for me."

Avery nodded and smiled at Amy before disappearing out of
the room.

"They do fill up a room, don't they?" Gwen looked at Amy,
sipping her tea. "Those two have always been close. I guess it's
because they are so much alike."

"I think it is so wonderful." Amy picked up her tea. "I wished
for this type of close loving family growing up." She swirled the
liquid in the cup. "I still do." She said softly.

"What was your childhood like, if you don't mind me
asking?" Gwen sat back against the cushions of the sofa.

"I want to lie and say normal. Full of family get-togethers, fun
holidays, and supportive sporting events," Amy told her. "But in
truth, I felt more like a prop than daughter, and the only events
like those I've mentioned were staged photo shoots."

"You didn't have any family vacations?" Gwen asked her.

"Oh, we have plenty of trips all over the world," Amy was surprised to hear the bitterness in her voice. "I guess most kids would love jetting off in a private jet or first class to exotic resorts and magical destinations. It would've been great if they weren't filled with photographers, camera crews, wardrobe people, make-up artists, personal assistants, and schedules."

"That sounds very stressful to put a child through." Gwen's voice was soft and warm. There were no traces of pity or scorn in it.

"It was," Amy admitted. "My hair could never be messy. I wasn't allowed to go splashing in raid puddles and I never got to choose what I wore."

"Never?" Gwen looked incredulous.

"Never." Amy sighed. "Even my pajamas were chosen for me by whichever au pair was following us around the world or looking after my brother and me at the time."

"When did you get to just be a little girl?" Gwen leaned over and took a sandwich.

"Whenever we went to visit my grandparent on their ranch just outside LA." Amy smiled remembering the ranch. "We spent most of our summer holidays with them."

"That's where you learned to ride?" Gwen smiled at Amy.

"Yes, and work the land." Amy poured herself some more tea and put honey in it. "They were my mother's parents and weren't into a celebrity life."

"Were they celebrities?" Gwen ate her sandwich.

"My gran was a producer at my grandfather's television network." Amy took a bite of her sandwich and finished chewing before she continued. "That is how they met, and it was love at first sight." She smiled. "My grandmother had my mother when she was in her mid-thirties. She worked right up until the day my mom was due and then stopped working to retire to her family's ranch and raise her daughter."

"That's such a lovely story." Gwen put her empty teacup on the coffee table.

"Yes, my mom and gran were total opposites." Amy sighed. "I never wanted to leave the ranch. While I was there, I had a normal loving family and did normal things."

"Then when you went back to LA it was back to being a prop?" Gwen guessed.

"Yes, my brother thrived on it. He wanted to be a talk show host like my mother," Amy explained. "So, he was groomed to take over her show one day. Which he did."

"What about your father?" Gwen kicked off her shoes and pulled her feet up onto the sofa.

"My dad was a bit warmer than my mom." Amy bit her lip. "When I was ten, he hurt his back and had to have an operation on it. After that, it caused him untold pain. The doctor prescribed him pain meds which he became addicted to. When the pain got too much that the meds wouldn't work, he started chasing the meds with bourbon. He said it was the only way to make the pain go away."

"I'm sorry, Amy." Gwen's eyes were filled with compassion. Amy gave her a small smile.

"The night of the accident that took his life when I was thirteen, was not the way the press and news spun it." Amy's voice dropped as did her eyes as she looked into the teacup. "He was drunk, passed out behind the wheel, the car swerved onto the wrong side of the road, and it was hit by a delivery van."

"Oh, Amy!" Gwen sat up, reached over, and squeezed Amy's arm. "That's awful."

"Luckily, the driver of the van wasn't badly injured. He was paid off to say that he was the one who fell asleep behind the wheel to save my father's reputation." Amy cleared her throat, swallowing down the tears threatening to spring out. "I was in the car with him and almost died too."

"I remember following your recovery from that accident," Gwen said softly, sitting back against the cushions. "I remember in a talk show a few years ago when you were asked about your peculiar on-set ritual of having everyone tested for substances.

You said because you knew first-hand the pain someone could cause by not being in control."

"I don't like alcohol or drugs," Amy said, waiting for the look of disbelief again from Gwen, but it didn't come.

"Amy." Gwen looked at her. "Have you ever thought about finding out who was drugging you?"

Amy looked at Gwen in shock at her words.

"You believe me?" Amy asked her, surprised.

"Of course," Gwen said. "Tammy told me many times that you were an advocate of anti-substance abuse campaigns."

"I tried to tell my brother that I was being drugged." Amy's eyes started to mist over.

It was the first time anyone had said they believed her. A person who'd welcomed her into her home and she didn't know that well was actually listening to her. For the first time, Amy felt she could be herself and tell her side of the story. There were no cameras or anyone looking for an edge or something to sell to the paparazzi.

"Sometimes, the ones closest to us are the blindest," Gwen told her. "They panic because they don't want to see their loved ones suffer."

"I guess." But still, Amy's heart couldn't let her forgive her brother's betrayal.

"Do you remember the times you might have felt strange?" Gwen asked her.

"I started a journal when I was in the rehab center and remembered as much as I could," Amy told her. "I kept it locked at all times because I wasn't going to have anyone read it. I thought it would tip whoever had done that to me off, and it would only give my therapist more ammunition to keep me in that place longer."

"That was wise," Gwen said. "Do you have the journal with you here in Montana?"

"As a matter of fact, I do." Amy smiled. "I was at the ski resort with my brother on a pretense of making amends with him and his girlfriend, who I'd blamed for drugging me."

"Oh," Gwen's eyes widened. "Did you accuse them outright?"

"I did." Amy nodded and sighed. "It was when I was first admitted to the rehab center and was in shock about what was happening." She swallowed. "I couldn't believe my life had been pushed into a corner like that. I had absolutely no control over it, and everything I said was taken as hostile or twisted to make me seem guilty of being an addict."

"That must've been so awful!" Gwen's eyes spilled over with tears and compassion for what Amy must've gone through.

"It didn't take me long to learn how to play the game, though." Amy cleared the emotion that was starting to clog her throat with a small cough. "But unfortunately for me, I learned it the hard way. My shock soon turned into disbelief, then hurt and feeling betrayed, before exploding in full force rage."

"Oh, dear!" Gwen watched Amy intently. "I can understand why you would burst with anger. I'm sure it was mostly fueled by frustration with having no one believe you or listen to you."

"I just kept thinking about some people who get accused of a crime they didn't commit, but no one will believe them or listen to them." Amy shook her head sadly. "It's what made me feel lucky to be in rehab and not a falsely accused criminal." She gave a mocking laugh. "Do you know how bad you have to feel to think of something like that?"

"Oh, Amy!" Gwen wiped a tear off her cheek. "My heart breaks for you."

"I've watched movies where things like what happened to me have happened to the main characters." Amy swirled her tea and watched it make a small whirlpool in the middle of the dark liquid. "It's not until it happens to you that you realize just how real and frightening it is that someone can manipulate your life or situation like that."

"It takes a person with a very black heart to do something so evil to another person." Gwen hissed. "I want to help you find out who did this to you, Amy."

"You know, even after a big heart-to-heart with my brother at the ski resort the day before the avalanche, I still believe he and

Ursula had been behind my drugging." Amy pushed down the pang of guilt that talking about her brother like that always gave her.

"Did your brother think you'd forgiven him?" Gwen's voice was soft.

"Yes." Amy nodded, feeling even guiltier. "But it was a lie." She looked up with Gwen, not bothering to hide the tears that blurred her vision.

"All that counts is that he believed it before he was taken from you." Gwen leaned forward and once again touched Amy's arm comfortingly.

"But it was a lie!" Amy sniffed and wiped at the tears spilling over her cheeks.

"Yet you wanted it not to be real," Gwen pointed out. "I can hear it in your voice. Your heart wants to believe he had no part in that heinous act. Once we've figured out who did it to you, you will be able to find peace and forgive him honestly."

"Yes, but it's too late." Amy's voice was barely a whisper. "How do I forgive him honestly now?"

"You let go of the hurt and anger boiling inside of you," Gwen told her. "Once your spirit if free of that anger it will set you mind free, and your heart will know where to find your brother."

"That's beautiful." Amy gave her another sad smile.

"Thank you. But you do know that before you can start to forgive your brother and let go you have to sort everything out first, Amy." Gwen smiled warmly at her. "There is no use in trying to reach out to clear your heart and your soul when your mind is so full of doubt and turmoil."

"Yes, you're right." Amy sighed. "Thank you, Gwen, for believing me and wanting to help me. I accept any help I can get with this. I didn't want to drag Tammy into this because she's had so much to deal with herself."

"I know. Your family has been through such heartache these past months." Gwen placed her cup on the coffee table and sat back. "If you tell me where your journal is, I will go get it for you. I think you should stay here as my guest. For a few weeks?"

"I don't want to put you out," Amy said.

"Have you seen how big this old house is?" Gwen laughed. "You are not putting us out at all, and our housekeeper, Nelly, will be thrilled to have someone else to cook for."

"Then I accept the invitation." Amy agreed without hesitation. "I think a break from Double A will do me some good."

"As soon as Avery and Ryan get home, I'll go back to Double A and speak to Tammy," Gwen offered. "Then I can get your journal, and tomorrow we can get started on our investigation." Excitement sparkled in her eyes.

"Don't you have enough on your plate with everything going on around the ranches?" Amy felt guilty plaguing Gwen with her problems.

"No, do you really think my overprotective little brother will let me get involved with that?" Gwen shook her head. "The only involvement he allows me or Avery to have is to keep us updated on the progress. He and some of the other family members of the five ranches have formed a group to investigate the problems."

"I believe Tammy, Chelsea, Cat, Maria, and Ashley have their own little group with Wallace helping them," Amy informed Gwen.

"Oh, really?" Gwen's eyebrows shot up in surprise. "Does Ryan's group know about that, I wonder?"

"I don't think so." Amy frowned. "Tammy's group seems to sneak around snooping on Ryan's group a lot."

"This is going to be fun after all!" Gwen grinned and quickly said. "I don't mean it as if the trouble is fun because that's bone-shaking frightening. But the two investigations will eventually collide, and that's bound to get some sparks flying."

"I know what you mean." Amy laughed. "I'm not involved in either group, so I hear both sides."

"You could be like a double agent." Gwen looked down at the teapot. "Can I get you any more tea?"

"No, thank you," Amy declined. "I've had two cups. It was delicious."

"I will take you through to the guest room where you'll be staying." Gwen stood up. "I asked Avery to get our housekeeper to get it ready for you."

Gwen helped Amy up, and she hobbled to one of the rooms on the ground floor.

"My parents used this room." Gwen smiled fondly as they walked into the huge room with the modern decorations. "I modernized it when my older brother, Todd, got married. But he wanted to stay in his room on the third floor. My father converted the loft into a one-bedroom flatlet for him when he turned eighteen, so he and Lynn stayed there."

"This room is beautiful, thank you, Gwen." Amy looked around the lovely bright room.

A door led through to a dressing room on the one side with the bathroom next to it. Large glass doors led onto a private veranda that looked out over the land to the sparkling river and mountains that loomed behind the house. Plush, slightly off-white leather furniture was arranged as a sitting area near the door. On the opposite of the room to the bathroom was a king-sized bed. The linen was white with dusky pink blankets and throw pillows on it. The color matched the heavy, white, and dusky pink curtains that hung beside the many windows in the room.

"You get settled in," Gwen told her. "I'll find out how far Avery and Ryan are. If you need anything, just shout."

Amy nodded and Gwen left her alone in the room, Amy sunk into the most comfortable mattress she'd ever felt, closing her eyes and drifting off to sleep. It had been quite a day.

# Chapter Seven

# AMY'S JOURNAL - PART 1

"Amy?" Gwen knocked on the bedroom door. "I have your stuff. May I come in?"

"Yes, of course," Amy called back.

Gwen walked into the room and found Amy lying on the bed. "Sorry, did I wake you?"

"No, I had just woken up and contemplated never leaving this comfortable mattress ever again." Amy grinned.

"It is a wonderful mattress," Gwen agreed. "I have them in all the rooms in the house."

"Oh, nice," Amy said. "Thank you so much for getting my stuff." She looked at the suitcase. "Did you find the envelope and my journal?"

"I did." Gwen put the case on one of the dressers. "Did you know that Jude knew you had your journal hidden beneath your bed at Double A?"

"I'm not surprised." Amy sighed. "He seemed to know everything going on in the house."

"That's because he's keeping the children and you are safe," Gwen stood up for Jude's actions. "Jude needed to know that anything you may be hiding wouldn't put your life in any more danger than it may already have been in."

"I suppose." Amy shrugged, trying to slide off the bed.

"What are you doing?" Gwen asked her with narrowed eyes.

"Getting up so I can unpack and get my journal. I think we should hide it and the envelope just in case," Amy suggested.

"I agree with you," Jude's voice startled them and made them turn to the open door. "Sorry, your door was open."

"Sure, it was," Amy said in disbelief. "What are you doing here, Jude?"

"Tammy and Greg asked me to come stay here as your bodyguard since Ryan saw someone watching you today," Jude explained.

"Great!" Amy's voice dripped with sarcasm. "Just when I was feeling secure here."

"Don't worry. Ryan put me in the room next door to yours." Jude ignored the sarcastic undertone.

"Doubly great," Amy hissed. "Am I to assume you also have listening devices set up in this room, so you know my every move?"

"It's just a precaution, Amy," Gwen surprised herself by siding with Jude again. "I will stay down here if you like, and Jude can move into a guest room upstairs."

"No, it's fine," Amy told her. "I won't feel bad about having Jude running around after me instead of you or Nelly."

"If that's what it takes to keep an eye on you, I don't mind." Jude gave her an angelic smile. "I'll help you out while your ankle heals." He glanced at the suitcase. "What I do need to know, though, is what is in that envelope and your journal that you needed so badly?"

"You really didn't look at any of it?" Gwen asked him in amazement.

"No." Jude shook his head. "I saw it was a journal, and the envelope was marked private, so I assumed it was just some papers Amy had. Like travel documents."

"Why would I hide travel documents under my bed?" Amy frowned at him.

"People hide their passports and travel documents in the

oddest places," Jude pointed out. "Are you going to tell me what's in there, or will I have to find out for myself?"

"Fine, if you must know..." Amy glanced at Gwen, who nodded.

"It's up to you if you want to tell him or not, Amy," Gwen told her. "I'll support you either way and..." She looked at Jude, and their eyes met, "You can trust Jude with security matters and secrets."

"I have been keeping a journal ever since I first thought I was being drugged," Amy told Jude. "The envelope contains information on my various blood work and the doctors that supposedly gave me prescription pain pills."

"Amy, why didn't you come to me about this before?" Jude stood staring at her with concern.

"Why?" Amy asked him. "No one except Gwen has believed that I was being drugged and never took the drugs that landed me in rehab."

"I have always wondered about that," Jude shocked both Gwen and Amy by saying. "I had always known and heard from your various bodyguards how anti-drugs you were."

"Are you serious?" Amy looked at Jude dumbfounded.

"I am," Jude nodded. "Can I see the evidence you have?"

Amy nodded and once again tried to get off the bed.

"No, you stay right there." Gwen stopped her and walked over to the dresser. "I'll get your diary and the envelope."

"Thank you, Gwen," Amy said. "I feel so helpless with this ankle."

"The more you rest, the quicker it will heal." Gwen opened the suitcase and pulled the items Amy wanted out. "Here." She handed them over to Amy before taking a seat on the bed.

"I tracked down the doctor whose name was on a few of the pill bottles found in my purse, car, and around my apartment," Amy told them, pulling out some documents from the envelope. "I don't even know who he is and why I'd be seeing him. He's a pediatric orthopedic surgeon. I didn't even know they could write prescriptions for such controlled pain medication."

"They can," Jude assured her, taking the documents she handed to him. "Can I keep these and go over them?"

"I..." Amy looked at Gwen.

"Why don't we both go over them in the study and let Amy rest?" Gwen suggested.

"Okay," Amy agreed. "I am still feeling quite tired and drained."

"I have to admit that my tea does have a relaxing effect on a person," Gwen admitted. "You need to get some rest."

"Here, take my journal as well." Amy yawned. "I trust both of you with it."

"Thank you." Gwen took Amy's journal. "You get some sleep, and I'll check in on you later."

Amy nodded, pulling the throw blanket back over her as she snuggled back into the pillows.

Gwen ushered Jude from the room, closing the door behind her.

"You don't need to get involved in this." Gwen pulled the envelope from Jude's hands before he had time to react. "I've got this, and I'm sure Amy would feel more comfortable with only me reading her journal."

"Oh, no, you don't!" Jude stopped Gwen from walking around him by stepping in front of her. "Amy is my responsibility. Anything that may be a potential threat or imminent danger to her is my business."

"He is right, you know, mom." Avery's voice had Jude stepping aside and spinning around to reveal her standing, watching them next to Ryan.

"How long have you two been standing there?" Gwen's eyes narrowed suspiciously.

"Long enough to know that something is going on with Amy that you two are keeping from us." Ryan walked forward.

"Yes, and if it puts Amy in any kind of danger, then it is also bound to impact our safety," Avery told them.

It was not until Ryan skillfully snatched both the journal and envelope from Gwen's hands that she realized Avery was distracting her and Jude for Ryan.

"Give that back, Ryan," Gwen warned him, her eyes narrowing dangerously at him. "Those are Amy's personal items, which she has not given either you or Avery permission to see."

"As the head of security operations for all the farms in our area, I also need to know about any potential threats to anyone residing here currently," Ryan pointed out smugly. "But I understand this is Amy's journal, so I will get permission from her to be involved with whatever is going on here."

"Really, you have enough on your plate with everything going on with the ranches, Ryan," Gwen said, trying to get the journal and envelope back from her brother.

"Nope!" Ryan stepped back. "These stay with me until further notice."

"Ryan, you don't know what you're doing," Jude hissed. "This is a very personal matter for Amy."

"Has this got anything to do with Amy's claims that she'd been drugged?" Avery shocked Gwen by asking.

"Why would you think that?" Gwen looked at her daughter questioningly.

"The date on Amy's journal is from when she was still in rehab," Avery pointed out as Ryan held the book with its cover facing out. "I'm a big Avery Guest fan." She shrugged at the three pairs of eyes staring at her.

"Amy is resting right now," Gwen told them, turning to Ryan. "Please give those items back to me until you have permission from Amy to help us."

"No," Ryan refused. "I'll hold onto these until then. Gwen, I don't want you or Jude getting involved in anything else potentially dangerous. It's bad enough that we have some unknown enemy stalking us."

"Actually, I think Wallace and his team have started to fit the pieces of what is going on together," Amy said from behind them.

Gwen and Jude turned to see her leaning against the door frame of her bedroom.

"You should be resting your foot!" Avery rushed forward to help support Amy and nearly collided with Ryan, who was going to do the same thing.

"You all need to learn to keep your voices down," Amy told them. "I was trying to rest."

"I've got her," Ryan told Avery, bending down to scoop Amy up into his arms.

"I can walk!" Amy objected.

"No, you really shouldn't," Avery pointed out. "I have an idea." She looked at Amy as Ryan set her gently down on the bed. "Why don't we get Nelly to bring us an early dinner up to Amy's room? We can sit in the lounge area going over your case."

"Is that your way of asking me if it's okay for you and your Uncle Ryan to help us with my investigation?" Amy laughed at Avery's subtle hint.

"Busted!" Avery grinned.

"Sure," Amy agreed. "I guess the more eyes I have on it, the better. Especially with me out of action for a few days."

"That's settled then," Avery said. "Mom, would you mind telling Nelly?" She looked at Gwen. "Uncle Ryan, can you get my laptop for research purposes?" She glanced at Jude. "You need to get settled into your room and let Ryan show you around."

"What are you going to do, Miss Bossy Britches?" Ryan's eyes narrowed at his niece.

"I need to do what I should've done the minute you brought Amy home," Avery told him. "I'm going to give her a complete examination." She looked at Amy. "I'd like to take you into Lewistown for an x-ray tomorrow."

"Do you think that's necessary?" Amy asked. Gwen noted the flash of panic in her eyes.

"Yes, Avery, do you think that's really necessary?" Gwen looked at her daughter.

"I do," Avery told them both and then looked at Amy. "Don't

worry. I'll be there with you the entire time." She gave Amy's hand a squeeze.

"I'll go in with you two to make sure," Jude told them before Ryan could offer.

"Good idea," Ryan told Jude, but Gwen could see the flash of anger in his eyes because he was going to offer to do it.

Gwen smiled to herself. Her little brother was a bit smitten with their guest, even if he would never admit it – not even to himself. While Gwen was happy to see him show interest in someone like that again after his divorce, she was also worried about him. Amy and Ryan were from two different worlds, and she didn't want to see them getting hurt when Amy decided to return to hers. Gwen knew Ryan was now home for good and would never move away from Four Lakes again. Not only did he love the ranch, but he had a strong sense of duty and family.

"Maybe leave Amy's items with her until we reconvene?" Avery suggested.

"I think I'll hang onto them," Ryan refused. "I know items such as these have been going missing lately. We are having problems trying to weed out who we can trust on the ranches and are not sure how many of our staff are now on whoever is doing this payroll."

"It's okay, Avery," Amy assured her when she saw Avery about to insist Ryan hand the items over.

"Let's leave Avery to make sure Amy is alright." Gwen ushered Jude and Ryan from the room. She turned back and smiled at Amy. "I'm so sorry about all this."

"Actually, it feels good to have so many people on my side for a change," Amy admitted.

Gwen smiled, nodded, and then backed out of the room, closing the door behind her.

"I hope you are both satisfied." Gwen looked at both men angrily. "Amy trusted me to help her, and now both of you nosey men have gotten involved." She looked from one man to the other. "Don't you both have enough on your plate with the ranch attacks?"

"Gwen, I saw someone stalking Amy," Ryan reminded her. "I went back to see if I could pick up the person's tracks, and there was nothing."

"Which means whoever is watching her is a professional," Jude continued for Ryan. "Now that we know Amy has been investigating her claims to being drugged, we have to consider that she's been watched because of that and not the ranch trouble."

Gwen sighed and closed her eyes for a few seconds. They were right, and Gwen knew it would be much better to have professionals help them. But still, this was supposed to be something she and Amy did together to help Amy. Not only to figure out what happened to her but also to help her get some closure and forgive her brother. Amy was carrying around a lot more than just anger over what had happened to her.

"You are both right," Gwen admitted, looking at them. "But don't you shut us out of the investigation. Amy needs to do this for far deeper reasons than just clearing her name."

"We won't!" Jude assured her, glancing warningly at Ryan.

"I promise we won't do that," Ryan said, although Gwen knew he was reluctant.

"If you do," Gwen warned them, "I will take Amy, and we will hire someone else to help us with the investigation."

"We've promised you we will not cut you out of this," Ryan told her. "But you must know that if things get dangerous, Jude and I will not let any of you step into the line of fire."

"Okay," Gwen nodded. "I guess, then, we understand each other."

Jude and Ryan nodded before following her down the stairs to carry out the assignments Avery had dished out.

<br>

*A*my was on the bed waiting for Avery to come back when there was a knock on her door.

"Come in," Amy called, expecting it to be Amy. She was surprised to see Ryan.

"Sorry, am I the first one here?" Ryan looked around the room.

"You are," Amy said, trying to control her heart that had gone wild the moment he stepped over the threshold.

"Can I help you to the sitting area?" Ryan offered.

"Yes, please," the words tumbled from Amy's lips before she had time to stop them.

She felt her cheeks heat up and her stomach flutter when Ryan bent down to scoop her into his strong arms once again.

"You really don't need to keep lifting me," Amy's voice sounded squeaky and strange to her. She cleared her throat quickly. "You're going to pull your back out at this rate."

"Nonsense." Ryan looked down at her. His hazel eyes seemed to burn into her soul and darken for a few seconds, but the emotion was gone before she could identify it. "You're light as a feather."

Amy didn't quite know what to say to that and was surprised to find her arms had somehow found their way to link around his neck. She was pulled close to his solid warm chest and could feel his heart beating against hers as he walked her to the sitting area. When he was about to set her down in the reclining chair, he and Jude had brought into her room earlier for her to raise her foot, their eyes locked. Amy felt drawn into the intense depth of his eyes as his head lowered towards hers. Before their lips could touch, a knock at her door broke the spell. They both pulled back so suddenly that Amy released her hold around Ryan's neck, and they nearly tumbled onto the chair.

"Watch out!" Jude rushed towards them.

Ryan managed to steady them before Jude reached them and gently deposited Amy into the chair.

"We're fine," Ryan assured Jude. "I stumbled over the rug," he lied and looked at Amy. "Are you okay?"

Amy knew there was a double meaning to his question and

didn't trust her voice at that moment, so she nodded, hoping Jude didn't notice her hot cheeks.

"Do you have the journal and envelope?" Jude asked Ryan.

"No," Ryan closed his eyes and shook his head. "Sorry, I'll go get them."

Without another glance at Amy, Ryan turned and left her room. She watched him go. When Ryan closed the door, her eyes fell on the dresser, where she saw the envelope and her journal. Ryan had brought them. Her heart did another flip as she realized he needed to gather himself after their near kiss. Ryan had been just as shaken by the intense chemistry between them as she had. Before Amy could ponder over her and Ryan's connection, Gwen arrived with Avery hot on her heels. Ryan didn't return until fifteen minutes later, helping Nelly with the dinner. Amy did note how he discreetly picked up the journal and envelope from the dresser when he walked into the room.

"We've been waiting for you," Gwen told Ryan.

"I went to help Nelly," Ryan helped the housekeeper put the serving cart where they could access it easily.

"I'll bring up dessert and coffee later," Nelly told them before leaving the room.

"I did some research into the facility you were admitted to," Ryan said as he sat next to Amy in an armchair. "I found something rather interesting about it." He pulled a notepad from beneath the journal and envelope he'd put on the coffee table in front of him. "Two months before you were admitted, the place was bought by Division Four."

Amy saw the shock register on Jude and Gwen's faces.

"Why does that name sound so familiar?" Avery asked before Amy could.

"Because they are the same company that the men that tried to shoot Cat Sparrow worked for," Gwen told her.

"No way!" Avery's eyes widened before they met Amy's. "Why would Division Four go after Amy?" She looked at Ryan and then Jude. "She's not associated with the ranches."

"But her brother was," Ryan pointed out. "He was married to Tammy."

"Yes, but why go after Amy?" Gwen wanted to know as well.

"Probably to get her out of the way while they stole her father's network from her," Ryan guessed.

"I think you'll find in some of the paperwork I have in that envelope that Carlos only bought my brother's shares in the network." Amy pointed to the envelope. "I was very surprised to see I still owned half of it."

"I spoke to Aunt Tammy a little while ago about Carlos," Avery told them. "I wanted to know how much she knew about him taking over the Guests' television network. I was surprised to find out that Carlos was actually a nice guy."

"Why would you think otherwise?" Gwen asked Avery.

"Because I read how he'd ruthlessly taken over the television network he owned before buying the Guests one," Avery said.

"I looked into Carlos the minute Tammy brought his son, daughter, and mother-in-law to Double A to live." Jude put the file he was holding on the table. "From what Christina, his daughter, and Estelle, his mother-in-law, told me, he was an honorable man."

"The networks he acquired were all struggling and about to go bankrupt," Ryan read from the file he'd taken from Jude. "The man managed to save many of the current employees' jobs and turn the stations around to make them profitable once again."

"According to the information I found out from various sources in LA, Carlos had found out just how badly the current management Amy's brother had appointed was doing." Jude continued telling them all about his findings. "Amy's grandfather had somehow helped Carlos start a new life in LA, and Carlos didn't want to see the legacy of a man he'd admired go down in flames."

"So, he bought out my brother's shares and not mine," Amy's eyes misted. "Martin told me that Carlos had bought the network outright."

"Your brother probably didn't know." Gwen, who was sitting on the other side of Amy, reached over and patted her arm compassionately.

"Or your brother, Martin, was trying to manipulate you and control your finances, knowing that as long as he did, he could also spend your money." Ryan gave them another scenario to consider.

"Why must you always go to the dark side?" Avery rolled her eyes angrily at her uncle.

"I would rather Amy have all the scenarios to weigh up than her getting shocked to find out her brother was a controlling manipulator slowly siphoning off Amy's fortune." Ryan looked at his niece with a blank expression on his face. "Avery, I know I've been very protective over you as you grew up. But I also know I taught you long ago that life doesn't come sugar-coated or wrapped in pretty bows."

"Yes, I know!" Avery said through gritted teeth. "It is messy, hard, and will give you knocks worse than any blow to the head ever could."

"Ryan!" Gwen hissed at her brother. "You told that to my daughter?"

"I did," Ryan said at the same time Avery said, "He did."

"That's what my father used to say to us," Gwen looked at her daughter apologetically. "I'm so sorry my callous brother told you that."

"It's fine, mom," Avery smiled reassuringly at her mother. "Uncle Ryan and Grandpops were right to tell me that."

"Grandpops told you that as well?" Gwen's eyes widened in angry shock.

"Yeah, long before Uncle Ryan did," Avery informed Gwen.

"I personally think everyone should learn that lesson," Amy butted in. "It's the truth, and what Ryan said about me having scenarios – even the worst ones – to weigh up is something I have to do." Her heart felt heavy, thinking that her brother could've done anything so cruel to her. "Especially when I still don't know for sure if Martin knew I was being purposely drugged or if he was the one doing it."

"Still, in our country, people are innocent until proven guilty," Gwen reminded them all. "So, until we find evidence that proves the contrary, I think we should give Martin, may his soul rest in peace, the benefit of the doubt."

"I agree with mom," Avery raised her hand.

"I second that," Amy raised her hand too.

Jude and Ryan gave each other a frustrated but resigned look, nodding their agreement.

"Good, well, now that that's settled, let's have our dinner that is getting cold." Gwen made the plan. "Then we can get stuck into helping Amy figure out who put her into the rehab."

# Chapter Eight

# AMY'S JOURNAL - PART 2

They enjoyed their coffee while Gwen went through Amy's journal, reading out significant dates and events Amy had highlighted. Avery was researching all the doctors who had supposedly written scripts for the pain medication Amy had been allegedly addicted to. Ryan and Jude were examining the timeline of events while instructing Avery on what they needed to research or look up.

"Does anyone know who owns this Division Four company that keeps popping up?" Amy asked after they'd found out that the doctors whose names were on the prescriptions all worked for clinics that were also associated with Division Four.

"It's someone I cannot find any information on," Jude told them. "A man named Oswan Bjorn. No one knows much about him, and I can't find if he even exists."

"If he owns such a powerful company, surely there must be some information on him?" Avery frowned.

"Can I have a look at that document, please?" Amy asked.

"Sure," Jude handed her the sheet of information he'd printed off about Division Four.

"The company has been around for almost six decades." Amy looked up at Jude. "It is a Scandinavian textile company." Her brows creased. "I don't understand what a textile company would want with TV networks and ranch land."

"It seems to be expanding into other markets," Ryan explained, looking at the other half of the document.

"Like ranching?" Amy asked with a confused frown.

"Our ranches aren't the only thing the company is trying to acquire," Avery told them, turning her laptop around. "The company has been buying up properties all over the country."

"Why?" Amy asked, looking at the screen.

"I'm not sure, but it looks like they are moving into real estate," Ryan said.

"It's an anagram!" Amy said suddenly, excitement brimming her voice, she turned to Ryan. "May I use your pen?"

Ryan nodded and handed his pen over to her.

"What's an anagram?" Ryan craned his neck to see what Amy was doing.

"The name is Oswan Bjorn." Amy finished writing and crossing off the letters before showing Ryan, who was sitting next to her. "This name kept popping up when I was trying to investigate who was drugging me. It always struck me as odd, but I also have a terrible habit of making other names out of people's names around me."

"Avery does that with number plates," Gwen told her. "She has to try and make the numbers into letters."

Amy handed the paper to Ryan to see the one name Oswan Bjorn's name made that they would all recognize.

"No way!" Ryan looked at the rearranged letters of Oswan's name and looked up at Amy in amazement before saying to everyone else, "Guess who."

Ryan plopped the piece of paper on the coffee table.

"Jason Brown!" Gwen, Jude, and Avery read out the name on the paper all at once.

"If you're right about this, Amy," Ryan looked at her, "I think we have definitely found our invisible enemy."

"The question remains, though, as to why a tech millionaire

is coming after all of us." Gwen rubbed her temples. "What is his end game?"

"That is what we have to find out before he plays whatever his next hand may be," Jude advised.

"Agreed," Ryan looked at Jude.

"I heard Wallace's group, which includes Tammy, Maria, Cat, Chelsea, and Ashley, mention something about Jason Brown being responsible for the avalanche," Amy informed them and saw the shocked look on all their faces.

"Do you know about this?" Ryan looked at Jude, who shook his head.

"No, but then again, I've been kept in the dark about Wallace's business with Tammy and Greg. I'm just there to provide protection for the girls and Amy," Jude told them.

"We need to get Wallace over here immediately!" Ryan pulled out his phone and started scrolling through it.

"Don't you think it's getting a little late for him to come over?" Gwen looked at her brother questioningly.

"No, it's only seven," Ryan glanced at his watch. "Besides, I'm not going to call him. I'm sending him a message."

"And how does that make it better?" Gwen asked him.

"Mom, Uncle Ryan is right," Avery took her uncle's side. "We need to know what Wallace does. Especially as someone is stalking Amy." She glanced down at the table guiltily.

"What is it?" Gwen asked her daughter. "I know that guilty look of yours when I see it."

"I went to get Uncle Todd's horse, Villain, from the far pasture earlier this evening when I saw a glint in the distance." Avery looked up at her mother. "As soon as I turned towards it, I saw a man get up and start to run off. I jumped on Villain and rode after him."

"You rode bareback and without reins after a potentially dangerous man?" Gwen stared at her daughter in shock and then turned to Ryan.

Ryan was also staring at her in shock. "Please tell me you didn't chase him down!"

"I can't do that." Avery pulled an apologetic face. "I did manage to get a photo of the guy, albeit a shaky one." Avery pulled out her phone and found the picture. "I think he was a reporter, though, as he had a camera around his neck."

"Avery!" Ryan's face went pale as he looked at the picture. "Are you completely out of your mind?" He hissed. "That is a camera used for surveillance, and I'm pretty sure that bulge at his side is a firearm." He pointed to the picture and handed it to Jude.

"Even though we now know what Amy's stalker look like, he has seen you as well," Jude pointed out. "That puts you in a lot of danger, especially when we do not know who this man is or what his intentions are."

"Does anyone want to acknowledge how brave Avery was, despite having acted recklessly?" Amy smiled apologetically at Avery. "We now have a face to put to my stalker, thanks to her."

"Of course," Gwen was the first to say. "Honey, which was a very brave thing you did. But you must understand it was also reckless and dangerous. It was a shock to us because we don't want you endangering your life."

"I understand." Avery sighed. "I do admit it was reckless of me. But when I saw him, I got so angry that someone was spying on us in our own home. The anger overrode any fear I may have felt at first."

"Honey, you also know not to go riding without the proper equipment," Gwen said gently. "Have you forgotten what happened the last time you did that?"

"Trust me, sister, she's ridden like that a lot more since then," Ryan gave Avery a smug smile when she glared at him for snitching on her.

"Fine, if you want to snitch on me," Avery's eyes narrowed at Ryan. "I wonder if Amy would be interested to know what I found in your trunks in the storeroom?"

"You wouldn't dare!" Ryan's eyes narrowed in on Avery.

They stared at each other for a few seconds before Avery raised an eyebrow challengingly.

"Avery, I'm warning you…" Ryan couldn't finish his threat because his phone rang. "It's Wallace." He lifted the phone to his ear. "Hello?"

Amy watched Ryan get up and walk onto the balcony as he spoke softly to Wallace.

"I wonder what that is about," Gwen said, watching Ryan walk off the balcony and into the back garden.

"I'm sure he'll tell us if it's anything important," Avery told her mother.

"Avery, will you please forward that picture you took of the stalker to me?" Jude asked her. "I'll get Wallace to run it for us and see if he gets any hits."

"Sure," Avery nodded. "What's your number?"

Jude gave Avery his number, and she sent him the photo.

"I really don't want to bring any more trouble than you all have onto your ranch already," Amy told them. "I feel awful about this." She looked at Avery. "While I'm grateful and think you are very brave, please, Avery, don't pull anything like that again."

"I won't," Avery promised.

"Wallace wants us all to attend a meeting tomorrow." Ryan walked back into the room. "I told him Amy was injured, and she needed to be included as she may just have found our enemy. He also thinks they are onto something." He took his seat next to Amy once again. "They are all coming here at ten tomorrow morning."

"Ryan, I wish you wouldn't do things like that without first consulting me," Gwen said, annoyed. "Poor Nelly is the one that gets the brunt of it because now she has to prepare all the snacks."

"Wallace said that Cupids Bow would supply the snacks," Ryan told her.

"I will do the refreshments such as coffee, teas, soft drinks, and water." Nelly surprised them by walking into the room to collect the dessert and coffee items. "If you've finished, I would like to retire for the night."

"Of course, Nelly," Gwen stood up to help her. "Please, leave this. I know it is past your down time."

"Oh, no bother." Nelly smiled warmly at Gwen. "I was making pies anyway."

"Cherry or peach?" Avery's eyes lit up.

"Both, and apple," Nelly told her. "But now I'll use them for the guests tomorrow."

"Aw, come on!" Avery moaned.

"I'll make you a deal," Nelly looked down at Avery, who was sitting on the floor in front of her laptop. "You clean up the coffee and dessert plates. I will save your favorite pie for you."

"You made my favorite pie?" Avery's eyes widened. "Deal!" She said instantly.

"Great, then I will say goodnight." Nelly turned and left amid a chorus of thank you and goodnights.

"I've sent the picture Avery took of Amy's stalker to Wallace to find out if he gets any hits," Jude told them.

"Let's see what he comes back with," Ryan said. "In the meantime, I think you and I need to patrol the grounds tonight." He looked at Jude. "You're down here next door to Amy, right?"

"Yes." Jude nodded. "I'll do some rounds during the night as well."

"Make sure this door is locked and bolted." Ryan pointed to the double doors that were open onto the patio.

"I will do that," Amy said.

"That's okay," Jude told her. "I'll do it for you."

"I can do it!" Amy felt a little annoyed that they didn't think she could lock a freaking door by herself. "I'm sorry to be rude." She stifled a yawn. "But I have a bit of a headache and would love to have a bath and then climb into bed."

"Of course." Gwen was the first to her feet. "Avery, will you take out the coffee cups and dessert plates." She looked at her daughter with raised eyebrows, "Like you promised Nelly?"

"On it." Avery jumped up, closed her laptop, and picked up

Amy's journal. "Do you mind if I take this with me and finish going through it with all the evidence you've gathered?"

"Not at all." Amy gave her a tired smile.

"Can I stay and help you?" Gwen offered.

"No, I'll be okay." Amy let Ryan help her up before her said goodnight and left the room.

When he was gone Amy felt a little cold and alone inside. She shook the feeling off and allowed Gwen to help her to her wardrobe to get her pajamas out and didn't even notice that Jude had closed and bolted the glass doors along with the heavy drapes.

"Night, Amy," Jude said, walking to the door. "You have my number in your phone, and I'm just next door if you need me."

"Thank you, Jude." Amy watched him nod and leave her room with Ryan.

Gwen checked her ankle one last time before saying good night and leaving with the tea tray.

"Are you sure you don't want me to stay and help you with your bath?" Gwen asked her.

"No, I've taken up enough of your time today, Gwen," Amy smiled at her. "I'll be fine."

"Okay, then, goodnight, Amy. Sleep well." Gwen left the room, pulling the door shut behind her.

Amy sat on the edge of the bed for a while, staring at the closed door before hobbling to the shower. She was going to go into Lewistown with Avery tomorrow afternoon to get x-rays and an orthopedic boot for her foot. Avery said it would help her become a little more mobile.

Amy felt too drained and tired to run a bath, so she jumped into a hot shower before putting on her pajamas and crawling into the comfortable bed. Amy's eyes drifted shut almost the minute they hit the pillow. As she drifted off, she found herself following the most beautiful red wolf she'd ever seen deep into the world of dreams. The animal was alarmingly large with the most amazing golden eyes she'd ever seen and large fangs, but she was not afraid. On the contrary, she'd never felt safer.

As they walked deeper into the realm of sleep, Amy knew he was communicating with her in his own way. The message he was sending her was to stay on the path fate had set for her and not try to fight it. There were times when she'd feel lost as she ventured into new unknown territory, but she needed to trust her instincts. And whenever she was feeling scared, doubtful, or alone, all she had to do was find the big red wolf. He'd been waiting patiently for her to arrive so he could guide her safely home where she belonged.

While they walked side by side, they stopped at the edge of a beautiful river. It's clear, fresh mountain water sparkled like diamonds in the warm sunlight. Thirsty, Amy kneeled on the banks to take a sip. But before she could dip her hands into the water, she was pulled away, and someone shouted her name warningly from the other side of the river.

Fear pounded through Amy's heart as she spun around to see a dark hooded figure descend upon her. Its large, beefy, gloved hands wrapped tightly around her upper arms as they yanked her to her feet. Again, her name was shouted from across the river, but Amy couldn't turn around to see who was shouting frantically for her. They sounded like they were pounding on the banks of the river, trying to get her attention. But Amy couldn't turn around. She was being held in the tight grip of her hooded assailant.

A deep warning growl rumbled from beside her as the shouting and thumping grew louder. The growl turned into a horrible feral sound of a beast attacking its prey. There was a blood-curdling scream, and the hands that held her arms in a vice grip fell away. Amy sat up, and a cold blast of air hit her like someone had doused her with ice water. Her eyes flew open at the same time her bedroom door burst open. Amy's head shot to the side, her eyes trying to adjust to the light pouring in from the passage to her dark bedroom.

"Amy..." Ryan's deep voice was low, and she heard a warning in it. "Stay very still."

"What?" Amy's brow crinkled into a frown. She wasn't sure if she was still dreaming or if this was really happening.

She was about to move when Jude's voice came to her from the opposite of the room from Ryan, "Listen to him, Amy."

"What is going on?" Amy croaked. Her throat felt dry like she'd swallowed sea sand.

Amy looked towards the open glass door and froze. Her eyes opened wide as she saw large gold eyes glowing at her from the open glass door. It was a wolf. But not just any wolf. It was the one from her dreams, and that's when Amy felt the pain in her upper arms. She looked down at them, but she couldn't see much in the dark. Amy heard the cocking of a trigger, and her head flew toward where Jude stood against the wall near the doors. Her eyes adjusted to light enough to see he had a gun and was aiming at the wolf.

"NO!" Amy shouted and sprung out of bed. Luckily, she landed on her good foot, and without a care for the pain shooting through her injured ankle, she positioned herself between Jude and the wolf.

"Amy!" Ryan shouted and started forward and then suddenly stopped. The wolf moved toward Amy, turning to growl at him. "Easy, boy." He held up his hands as the wolf sidled closer to Amy.

"Please, let him go!" Amy said, holding her hands in front of her as she slowly turned toward the animal that was a lot closer to her than she'd thought. "Please, trust me on this. You need to let him go. Just step aside Jude and he'll go."

Amy looked back down at the wolf she was now almost face to face with. Her heart thudded in chest as their eyes met. They were the same golden eyes she'd seen in her dream, and her breath caught in her throat. Amy stood frozen to the spot, holding her breath. Although she didn't know what to do, Amy somehow knew the wolf would not harm her. After a few heart-stopping seconds, the wolf turned and ran out the glass doors. Amy turned to watch him disappear into the night. That was not the only thing she saw. Her eyes dropped to the ground, where she saw drops of blood leading out of her room onto the patio.

"Are any of you hurt?" Amy turned around to look at Jude and was nearly blinded when Ryan switched on her bedroom light.

She saw nothing but black spots in front of her eyes and, without thinking, took a step onto her sore ankle. Before she toppled onto the floor, Ryan rushed forward and caught her.

"Are you hurt?" Ryan sounded breathless as he carried her to her bed.

As he was setting her down, Gwen, Avery, and Nelly ran into the room.

"Can we come in now?" Avery stopped when she saw Ryan tenderly looking over Amy's limbs for injuries. "I'll do that, Uncle Ryan." She walked over, but Ryan shook his head.

"She's not injured," Ryan assured Avery.

"I have a terrible taste in my mouth and a burning sensation in my nose," Amy told them.

"I think that would be because someone was trying to chloroform you." Jude bent down and picked up a rag lying next to her bed which he sniffed then pulled face.

"Are you or Ryan hurt?" Gwen asked, looking at the same spots of blood Amy saw on the floor.

"No, I'm not." Ryan shook his head and looked at Jude.

"No, neither am I." Jude went over to where Gwen was standing. But that is definitely blood."

"You didn't hurt him, did you?" Amy looked at Jude accusingly.

"Hurt who?" Avery frowned.

"The big red wolf with the golden eyes." Amy saw the shock on Avery's face as she stared at Amy.

"Did you say big red wolf with gold eyes?" Avery repeated and swallowed.

"Yes." Amy nodded. "He was in my room." She frowned. "I think he saved me."

"The blood trail goes that way." Jude followed the spots past

Gwen and out onto the patio. "How the heck did the intruder get inside? I know I locked and checked Amy's door."

"These doors are unfortunately quite easy to open," Ryan explained. "We need to reinforce them with bolts on the top and bottom of each door." He walked to the patio and looked at the one door. "I'll get it done tomorrow."

"I think we need to move Amy upstairs," Gwen said. "I don't like her being down here." She looked at Jude. "There are two rooms next to each other upstairs that I will get Nelly to set up later today."

"Today?" Amy frowned and glanced at the big clock on the wall. It was just after midnight.

"I know you are in a strange house." Ryan looked toward Amy. "But please, can I ask you not to lock your bedroom door in case we need to get in like we did tonight?"

"I never locked the door," Amy told him. "The last person near the door was Gwen when she closed it."

"And I never locked it!" Gwen held up her hands.

Amy caught the look that passed between Jude and Ryan.

"What?" Amy asked them.

"Amy, I don't want to panic you, but this rag had chloroform on it." Jude looked awkwardly towards Ryan for his input.

"They think someone was trying to kidnap you." Avery's eyes narrowed as she looked from Jude to Ryan. "Until Goldie saved you."

"Goldie?" Jude, Gwen, and Ryan all said at once, staring at Avery in amazement.

"Uh..." Avery started to back away from them. "I have a sleeper couch in my room. I'll sleep on that, and Amy can sleep in my bed tonight until Nelly can get the other spare room done." She shifted the conversation back to Amy.

"Oh, no, you don't!" Ryan raised his eyebrow at his niece and blocked her exit. "Avery, do you have another red wolf friend you haven't told us about?"

"Another wolf friend?" Amy frowned and looked at Avery, who gave her a quick smile.

"Yes, I used to have a wolf named Big Red when I was younger," Avery told her. "He saved my life!" She raised her voice a little bit to get her point across. "Big Red and Uncle Ryan became very close after that."

"I thought all the red wolves died when Big Red did?" Gwen said.

"Uh..." Avery bit her bottom lip and looked sheepish. "Not exactly."

"Avery..." Ryan looked at her warningly. "What did you do?"

"Why do you immediately think I've done something?" Avery shook her head in disgust.

"Because you have a guilty look on your face," Ryan told her.

"Okay!" Avery said. "Not long after Big Red died, I found a litter of red wolf pups."

"Why didn't you say anything?" Gwen asked her.

"You were away a lot with your businesses. Uncle Ryan lived in California because of his military career, and Uncle Todd was busy with the ranch and his security firm," Avery explained. "His wife had just left him, and he'd just thrown himself into his work." She twirled a stray lock around her finger. "I couldn't find the pups' mother at first, and they were so hungry and tiny. I deduced they must've been Big Red's litter as he would've died when his mate was only a few weeks pregnant."

"Avery, did you adopt a litter of feral wolf pups?" Gwen looked at her in shock. "Honey, you know they could've had all kinds of diseases, including rabies."

"Gwen!" Ryan frowned at his sister. "When did you last hear of a rabies outbreak in our area?"

"There was that outbreak in Big Horn County not so long ago," Gwen pointed out. "That's only about three hours away."

"Mom, these pups were born long before that." Avery gave a small laugh. "Anyway, only one of the pups survived. I didn't take them the day I found them. I figured Delphine, Big Red's mate, would come back for them soon." She looked down at the floor as a cloud of sadness filled her eyes. "I found Delphine the next day. It was a horrible sight. She'd been caught and skinned by poachers."

"Who is Delphine?" Ryan frowned questioningly.

"Big Red's mate," Avery said impatiently rolling her eyes at Ryan. "Really, Uncle Ryan you need to keep up."

"Oh, honey." Gwen went to her daughter and engulfed her in a hug. "I'm so sorry."

"I called Uncle Zac immediately, and he came with his wildlife crew to take her way." Avery continued her story. "I immediately went to find the cubs, but only one was still alive."

"Let me guess, that was Amy's recent guest, Goldie?" Ryan looked towards the door.

"Yes," Avery nodded. "Uncle Zac and I have tried to find him a mate over the years, but he's never been interested in any of them."

"Are you telling me there are stray wolves running around in the mountains that you and Uncle Zac have set free?" Ryan's eyes narrowed.

"No." Avery shook her head. "We put them in a large, specially-made pen."

"You more than anyone should know that's not how wolves chose who they have as their partner." Ryan sighed. "We'll take this Goldie situation up at another time." He looked at Amy. "Are you happy to stay with Avery for what's left of the night?"

"Yes," Amy nodded.

Amy wished she was brave enough to say she'd be okay down here. But she was far too shaken to act bravely.

"I'll get Amy up to Avery's room." Before Amy could protest, Ryan had already scooped her into his arms. "Sorry, but I don't think you should put any more weight on that foot."

Amy couldn't talk as her heart felt like it was trying to pound its way out of her chest, and she felt quite breathless, feeling Ryan's solid warmth against her again.

"I'll grab some of Amy's things," Avery offered and turned to her mother. "Are you and Jude okay to try and secure this room, Mom?"

"Sure, I will show Jude where he can get some planks or something to secure the doors," Gwen offered.

"We can do that," Jude answered for the both of them.

Ryan nodded and walked Amy out of the room, up the stairs, and into what Amy assumed must be Avery's room.

"Are you sure you're alright?" Ryan asked her as he gently laid her down on the big, rumpled bed.

"I'm fine, really," Amy assured him, touched by his concern. "I know this sounds strange..." She stopped herself and shook her head, "Never mind. It's silly."

"Try me." Ryan stood up and looked down at her with interest.

"I didn't feel afraid of Goldie at all." Amy looked up at him and then glanced down at her hands. "When I fell asleep, I dreamt about him. I was walking by his side, and I felt so safe for the first time in a very long time."

Amy frowned when she looked back up at Ryan and saw the look of shock on his face.

"Are you okay?" Amy's eyes widened with concern.

"What?" Ryan seemed to snap out of deep thought.

"You look shocked," Amy told him.

"Oh no," Ryan said. "I was just thinking about your dream. My mother would've told you that you'd finally met your spirit guide.

Before she could ask him what he meant, Avery walked into the room.

"Well, that's my cue to leave." Ryan walked to the door. "Remember we have that meeting at ten," he told them before disappearing.

# Chapter Nine

# SOME THINGS ARE MEANT TO BE

Avery lay on the sleeper couch she'd pulled next to her bed, staring up at the ceiling as she told Amy the story of Big Red and his mate Delphine.

"So, you introduced Big Red to Delphine?" Amy turned on her side to look at Avery in the soft yellow glow of the bedside lamplight.

"Yes, myself and Uncle Zac found her at a zoo of all places." Avery shuddered. "I think it was love at first sight between her and Big Red."

"Was her name already Delphine?" Amy asked.

"No, she didn't have a name." Avery looked toward Amy. "They called her wolf five."

"How awful." Amy shook her head in disgust. "I hate zoos."

"Some do a lot of good and go to a lot of trouble to provide the animals with a habitat that suits them." Avery put her hands behind her head and looked up at the ceiling once again. "Not that one, though, and the horrible thing was that although Delphine was wolf five, there were no other wolves there."

"I hope you got that zoo closed down." Amy felt the anger bubble up inside her.

"That was the reason we were able to get Delphine. The zoo was being forced to shut down due to animal neglect and cruelty." Avery stifled a yawn. "I'm sorry if Goldie scared you tonight."

"I admit I was petrified, but at the same time, I knew I wasn't in any imminent danger," Amy admitted. "I was telling Ryan about it just before you walked in."

"Oh?" Avery turned her head to look at Amy.

"Yes. It was the strangest thing." Amy felt almost compelled to tell Avery about her dream right up to when she'd jumped between Jude and the wolf he was about to shoot.

"You dreamt about a big red wolf?" Avery bit her lip contemplatively. "Was it leading you home?"

"Yes!" Amy frowned. "Ryan told me that his grandmother would have said I'd just met my spirit animal."

"My great-grandmother loved wolves and used to study them," Avery told her. "There used to be quite a lot that roamed this valley once."

"How interesting." Amy flopped over onto her back. "And you? How did you become interested in wolves having a saved a few?"

"I've always just loved all animals. When I met Big Red, we bonded and I fell in love with the creatures. And Uncle Ryan was right, though about your dream. You may just have met your spirit animal for the first time tonight." Avery turned over onto her side, facing Amy. "Mine and Uncle Ryan's spirit animals are also wolves."

"So, we're like a wolf pack?" Amy grinned and turned her head to see Avery smile.

"I guess so," Avery agreed. "I wonder where the home is that your wolf was leading you to?"

"That was the strangest thing." Amy frowned. "It was like I was already where I was supposed to be physically and that it wasn't a physical home, he was leading me to."

"Maybe he was leading you to your soul mate?" Avery's eyes widened excitedly. "Sorry, I didn't even ask. Do you have anyone special back in LA?"

"No." Amy shook her head. "I've had a few failed long-term relationships. But nothing that ever ended in a permanent one." She sighed. "I guess I just haven't met my soulmate yet."

"But I think you may just be going to meet him if you haven't already." Avery flipped back over on her back. "Maybe it's Jude." She turned her head to Amy and grinned. "He's not bad for a man in his mid-fifties."

"Good grief, no!" Amy stated. "Besides, I have seen how he and your mom look at each other." She frowned once again. "They seem to have a history." She looked at Avery. "Do you know anything about that?"

"No." Avery shook her head. "But I've also noticed how they look at each other and how much my mother does everything to avoid being alone with him."

"Has your mother dated since your father passed away?" Amy asked Avery. "Sorry, do you mind if I ask that question?"

"Not at all," Avery said. "And no, I don't think she's even gone on one date, even though both my uncle Todd and I tried to encourage her to do so."

"That is sad because she is such a beautiful person both inside and out." Amy's eyes narrowed. "Maybe we need to find out what is up between her and Jude?"

"I don't think that's a good idea," Avery said. "My mom is a very private person, especially about dating."

"Fair enough, but that doesn't mean we can't still help nudge her and Jude together in the right direction." Amy looked at Avery apologetically once again. "Sorry, I hope I'm not stepping on any sensitive issues."

"Not at all." Avery shook her head. "I'd like nothing more than to see my mom settle down with such a nice guy as Jude."

"Don't tell him I said this because I'll deny it," Amy lowered her voice, "But he deserves someone special in his life after everything he went through with his first wife."

"I believe she died from injuries sustained in the line of duty." Avery's eyes darkened in sympathy. "But she'd been in a coma for five years before she passed away."

"How did you know all that?" Amy looked at Avery, surprised.

"Aunt Molly, Tammy's aunt told me yesterday afternoon." Avery grinned. "She also asked me how I felt about my mom ever getting married again."

"That was a strange thing for her to ask you." Amy frowned.

"I think she was hinting at something between my mom and Jude." Avery suppressed another yawn.

"You're tired," Amy pointed out. "I think we should try and get another few hours of sleep before we have to get up."

"Oh wow, it's already nearly two-thirty." Avery looked at the clock on the wall. "We can still sleep for another three to four hours."

"Sounds good to me." Amy rolled over and switched off the bedside lamp. "Night, Avery."

"Night, Amy," Avery said back. "Amy, if you dream of your wolf again, let him lead you to where you need to go. Sometimes our dreams can help us with whatever is troubling or confusing us."

"I will give it a try," Amy promised, turning over and closing her eyes.

When Amy started drifting off to sleep, she called for the big red wolf with the gold eyes, and to her surprise, he came. This time Amy reached out to it and stroked its fur, letting him know she understood who he was now and that she trusted him as her guide. As they walked down a grassy path, the fields beside them changed to one sprinkled with blue daisies. The path changed and became steep, but her wolf helped her climb it. When she stumbled, he steadied her and made sure she didn't fall. But by the time they got to the top of the hill, Amy felt more exhilarated than tired. The land once again flattened out at the top even though there were still a lot of obstacles Amy had to navigate. But she pushed on, led by her trusted guide as she followed the calling of her heart and a peculiar longing she had started feeling in her soul. Just before Amy dropped into a very deep sleep where dreams stopped and her body shut down to restore itself, another face with hazel eyes and jet-black hair drifted into her thoughts.

※

*R*yan paced back and forth as he listened to Wallace on the phone.

"Are you sure this is correct?" Ryan asked him, feeling perplexed. "Is the meeting still on for ten?"

He glanced at his wristwatch. It had just turned eight.

"Okay, I'll see you then." Ryan hung up and pinched the bridge of his nose. A knock at the study door caught his attention. "Come in."

Jude walked into the room. "You sent a message for me to come see you?"

"Yes." Ryan nodded and pointed to the seat in front of the desk. "I got some information back from Wallace."

"Did he get a hit on the photo we sent him?" Jude sat down.

"Yes, but he is still waiting for the lab results on the blood sample I took to him in the early hours of this morning," Ryan told him.

"Did you get any sleep at all last night?" Jude asked.

"No, did you?" Ryan sent the question back to Jude.

"No," Jude admitted. "I did see Avery's wolf sleeping in one of the paddocks."

"I feel oddly more at ease knowing that." Ryan looked at his phone.

"It is like having a wild watchdog around." Jude glanced at Ryan's phone as he slid towards him.

"The stalker that Avery managed to get a photo of is Winston Brown." Ryan tapped next to the phone, pointing out the information. "He and his family used to live in Lewistown. His father died, and he had to go live with an aunt of his until he graduated high school the following year."

"Is he related to Jason Brown?" Jude looked up at Ryan.

"Yes, Winston is Jason's father." Ryan sat back in his chair. "Wallace's team managed to find out that Winston works for—"

"Division Four," Jude guessed, and Ryan nodded in confirmation. "Ursula Duggal, who we suspect was working with Jason Brown, was arrested for accessory to murder. She too had ties to Division Four."

"Isn't she the woman Tammy's husband was having an affair with?" Ryan frowned.

"Yes, she was." Jude pushed Ryan's phone back to him and told him the story that Christina Santiago, Tammy's new house guest, had told them about Ursula.

"Some people really don't deserve to be parents," Ryan muttered angrily. "I have a feeling that this is what Wallace wants to discuss today."

"Do you think that Winston Brown broke into Amy's room last night?" Jude sat back in his chair and looked at Ryan thoughtfully.

"I don't know him or what he is capable of," Ryan said. "Wallace is still trying to get some more information on Winston."

"Did you know Winston?" Jude rubbed his chin.

"No, he was a year or two ahead of me." Ryan frowned. "I think he was in the same year as Maria Parker or maybe Tammy." He shook his head. "His sister was also at our school. Everyone knew who she was as Bronwyn Brown was head cheerleader and the high school prom queen mean girl." His brows drew together. "Bronwyn used to date Greg Watson."

"Oh!" Jude didn't sound too surprised. "Wasn't he the high school quarterback?"

"Yes," Rayan confirmed. "I guess it was fitting the two of them dating!"

"Is Greg going to be at the meeting today?" Jude looked at Ryan thoughtfully. "Maybe he knew Winston?"

"I believe he is." Ryan leaned forward and picked up his phone. He scrolled through is message Wallace had sent him about the meeting later that morning. "Wallace also said that two new people would be accompanying Greg."

"Let's hope Wallace has finally pieced everything together." Jude shook his head. "Everyone around here has been living on edge for far too long."

"If this has all been about some sort of grudge of revenge," Ryan's eyes narrowed. "If the Browns are really behind all this, they must really hate all of us for some reason that we don't even know about."

"So much that it's even spilled over to anyone associated with the five families, like Amy," Jude pointed out. "They are also so cunning that they found a way to rile up some of the ranch's employees by feeding them bogus information. Unfortunately, it has cost all those innocent people not only their jobs but some of them their freedom. Tammy's housekeeper, Constance, their longtime foreman, Pete, and all the others that have been rounded up."

"I know. It is really sad as most of the people that have turned against us have been with the five ranches for many years." Ryan ran a hand over his face. "Some of their fathers or mothers worked here as well."

"I was asked to look after Brynn and Amy after the avalanche because they were being watched while they were in Malibu," Jude told him, suddenly changing the subject as a thought struck him. "So that means that whoever this is, they have deep pockets and can get to anyone anywhere in America. Once again that dial seems to land on Jason Brown as we all know he has extremely deep pockets."

"There are still just so many pieces of the puzzle that don't seem to fit." Ryan leaned forward and picked up his notebook, which he leafed through. "I've been documenting all the incidents and bits of information I've been able to gather."

"And?" Jude's brow creased as he watched Ryan go through his notebook.

"Here, see for yourself." Ryan closed the book and handed it to Jude. "I've tried to put it all together on a time lime at the back of the book."

Before Jude could start going through it, there was a knock on the study door, and Gwen walked in.

"Good morning." Gwen's eyes darkened, and a warm smile spread across her lips when she looked at Jude, Ryan noted, shrewdly.

*Is there something going on between Gwen and Jude?* Ryan wandered with conflicting emotions. If there was, he was glad for his sister but at the same time how well did the two of them know each other. As far as Ryan knew they'd only just met when Jude came to look after Amy and Brynn at Double A ranch. He shook the thoughts away. Gwen was grown woman and he knew better than to interfere in her love life.

"Good morning to you." Jude's facial expression softened, and his voice dropped.

Ryan's eyes narrowed as he observed his sister and Jude. Something was definitely going on between them. Ryan didn't know whether to be happy about it or not. He'd never seen Gwen look at a man like she was looking at Jude. Well, not since Reece, her late husband, but that was decades ago. She deserved to be happy, but what worried Ryan was that Jude lived in LA and what would happen after he was no longer needed here?

Ryan was about to say something, but he stopped himself. It was not his place to interfere. All he could do was observe from afar and step in when or if needed.

"You two coming for breakfast?" Gwen asked. "Nelly is waiting for you both."

"Right!" Ryan stood up. "I'm starving."

Jude stood up as well and stepped towards Gwen. Ryan had to physically stop himself from stepping in between them when his protective instincts over his sister kicked in. Instead, he stood back and let Gwen and Jude leave the study before him. As he followed them to the dining room, Ryan didn't miss the subtle hand touches or whispers. They were like teenagers trying to hide their crush on each other. He shook his head and sighed to himself.

*It's none of your business, Ryan.* He gave himself a lecture before he walked into the dining room. *Keep your nose out of it.*

Ryan was soon distracted when he saw Amy sitting at the table, dressed in a pale pink and white snap-up cotton shirt with a light green bandana tied around her neck. Her thick golden hair was swept back into a ponytail while soft tendrils escaped and framed her beautiful face. When she saw him, she gave him a warm smile that made his heart thud so hard it nearly left him breathless.

*Good grief, man, get a grip!* Ryan gave himself a mental shake. *Talk about acting like a teenager with a freaking crush.*

Ryan greeted everyone around the table, trying not to make eye contact with Amy as he seated himself at the head of the table opposite Gwen.

"It is so lovely to have a table with more than you three, who are normally never in one place at the same time," Nelly said with a grin and looked at Amy. "I usually have to serve breakfast in three stages as Avery, Gwen, and Ryan are not normally here at the same time."

"I love having big family breakfasts," Amy admitted to Nelly.

"I hope you stay for a while, Amy," Nelly said. "My parents always believe that a family should have at least two meals a day together."

"I think Nelly is trying to make us feel bad." Ryan laughed. "But she is right. We do need to make more of an effort to have family meals."

"See, you are a good influence on my Gwen, Ryan, and even my darling Avery." Nelly kissed Avery on the head. "Now dig in and enjoy. Is there anything else you might want?" She looked from Amy to Jude.

"Nelly, if you're so into family meals, why don't you join us?" Avery challenged her with a smug smile.

"Because I've already had my breakfast, been for my walk, and now I have to supervise the cleaning staff." Nelly smiled at Avery. "But if you all got up at least an hour and a half earlier, I would."

With that, Nelly left the dining room, and they started to discuss the events of the previous night, and then Avery talked about Goldie. It was nice to have some normalcy after everything happening around them. Nelly was right. It was nice to sit down for a meal with family. She wasn't sure, however, about Amy's influence on him.

# Chapter Ten

# THE MEETING - PART 1

Amy sat next to Gwen on the sofa and rested her injured foot. She felt bad that the meeting venue had to be changed because of her, even though no one seemed to mind.

"It's been a long time since we've been to Four Lakes," Cat Sparrow said to Gwen.

Cat was seated on the larger sofa. She was wedged between Maria Parker and Chelsea Hitchin, while Tammy was on the one side of the sofa, and Ashley on the other, each in chairs Nelly had positioned around the living room for the meeting. Amy hadn't been at the last meeting the ranches had had. Although she'd been introduced to many people there, Amy hadn't spent time with any of them. She had felt like a stranger until Tammy arrived with Greg. A petite brown-haired woman and a man who was a mirror image of Greg were with them.

Tammy immediately walked over to Amy to find out how she was.

"I've been so worried about you," Tammy said, leaning down to embrace her.

"Gwen and her family have been taking great care of me." Amy smiled up at Tammy. "I just feel like such a burden because my new doctor." She pointed to Avery, who was chatting to

Liam, Maria's son, who was also a doctor, "Insists I keep off my foot for at least two to three more days."

"You're in the best hands with Avery," Tammy assured her. "I have it on excellent authority that she is a great doctor."

"Hi, Amy." Greg bent down to hug her as well. "I'm glad you are okay."

"Thank you." Amy smiled up at him. "Did you make a clone of yourself?" She looked pointedly at the man standing behind him with his arm wrapped around the woman he'd arrived with.

"Oh, no!" Greg rolled his eyes. "Watts," he called the man closer. "This is Amy, Tammy's sister-in-law."

"I don't need an introduction!" He took Amy's hand, leaned down, and kissed it gallantly. "I would know the amazing Amy Guest anywhere. Besides, she acted in at least two of my movies."

"Your movies?" Amy frowned up at the man after he straightened, and she took her hand back.

"Watts is my brother, and you would know him as Grayson Wyatt." Before Greg could finish, Amy nodded and looked at Watts. "This lovely lady beside him is his wife, Bronwyn."

"Hi," Amy greeted Bronwyn, who greeted her back before Amy looked up at Grayson, saying, "It's an honor to finally meet the elusive Grayson Wyatt." She frowned. "But why does your brother call you Watts?"

"It's an awful childhood nickname that I've long since outgrown, but my brother and friends back in Hicksville here have not." He shook his head. "I have tried on many occasions to get them all to stop calling me that, but I have long since given up," his eyes scanned the room where Zac Sparrow, Brett Parker, and West Lockran were taking a seat facing everyone else, "trying to get them to call me Grayson."

"You should just ignore them then when they call you Watts," Amy suggested. "They'll soon have to start calling you by your real name.'

"That is an excellent idea." Grayson raised an eyebrow at his brother, who shook his head and rolled his eyes again.

"This may sound like an obvious question, but are the two of you twins?" Amy looked from Grayson to Greg.

"We are," Grayson grinned. "With me being the eldest."

"Why do you always have to rub that in?" Greg shook his head at his brother before saying something to Tammy, giving her a kiss. "Excuse me, I have to go take my seat with those guys." He pointed to Brett Parker, Zac Sparrow, Wallace, and West Lockran who were seated all together facing the rest of the people in the living room.

"Where do you want us to sit?" Grayson asked Greg.

"You are welcome to join us," Gwen said from beside Amy and stood up to greet them.

"Oh, shoot, sorry," Amy felt awful for not introducing Gwen. "This is..."

"Gwen Beckett!" Grayson smiled at her and treated her hand to a kiss as well. "You are still as lovely as ever."

"And you are still the charmer, I see." Gwen smiled back at him and then looked at Bronwyn. "Hi, Bronwyn. It's been a long time."

"Hello, Gwen." Bronwyn embraced her.

"How is your mother?" Amy heard Gwen ask Bronwyn softly.

"Struggling, but still a fighter," Bronwyn told her.

"Come sit in these two chairs beside the sofa." Gwen pointed to the chairs.

Soon everyone was seated in the Four Lakes living room. Zac, Brett, Greg, West, and Wallace sat facing the rest of the people in the room.

"We've asked you all here today as it has come to our attention that we have quite a few different groups investigating the troubles that have affected all of us here today." Greg started the meeting. "It will not get us anywhere if we all keep holding pieces to what has been a very frustrating and perplexing mystery to ourselves instead of putting them together."

"Yesterday, Ryan noticed that Amy was being followed, and last night someone tried to break into her room right here at

Four Lakes," Wallace continued, and all eyes turned to Amy, making her squirm.

"Oh, my word Amy!" Tammy, who was sitting in an armchair next to Amy, looked at her wide-eyed. "Why wasn't I told about this right away?"

"It happened at midnight," Amy said softly. "I was fine thanks to..." She stopped herself from saying wolf, "Jude, Ryan, Gwen, and Avery."

"Do you have any idea what the perpetrator was looking for or wanted?" Tammy looked toward Ryan and then Jude.

"Amy!" Jude and Ryan startled Tammy by saying together.

"Excuse me?" Tammy's eyes widened in shock. "Do you mean to tell me someone tried to abduct Amy from her room here at Four Lakes?"

Ryan, Jude, Gwen, Avery, and Amy all nodded.

"I managed to get a picture of the guy, who we think has been stalking Amy," Avery told everyone. "Jude sent it to Wallace, who managed to get an ID on him."

"Do we know the person?" Tammy turned to look questioningly at Wallace.

"It was Winston Brown!" Wallace's eyes moved to Bronwyn, who gasped.

"Winston is back here in the Lewistown area?" Grayson said through gritted teeth. His hand captured Bronwyn's, who immediately sat closer to him.

"Yes," Greg nodded, looking worriedly at his brother and Bronwyn. "I don't think it is safe for either of you to be back here."

"You were the Grayson that Pete and his group who kidnapped Grace wanted?" Maria said, staring at Grayson.

"Excuse me?" Grayson frowned, and his head shot around to his brother. "Someone kidnapped Grace?" He looked at Greg, shocked.

"Yes," Maria answered before Greg could. "When Greg asked them what they wanted so he could get his daughter back, they said Grayson."

"We didn't know who you were," Cat continued. "No one would tell us." Her eyes narrowed accusingly as she looked at Zac, Greg, West, and Brett.

"Ah." Grayson nodded. "I'm the family's deep dark secret." He laughed. "But seriously, there is a reason why Bronwyn and I have hidden from the world for so long."

"Greg, why didn't you mention Grace had been kidnapped?" Bronwyn's eyes were huge with fear. "Grayson and I would've come here sooner."

"Why are you here?" Chelsea asked them.

"Someone broke into our house and left a note for us on our foyer mirror," Bronwyn told them with a shudder. "It was a not-so-subtle invitation to return to Montana, stating we wouldn't like the consequences if we weren't back here within a week." She looked down at her hands. "My mother is quite ill and now. She is in a frail care center. We have been hiding for so long that I wanted however long she has left with us to be one lived in peace. Not this constant fear we've had of my half-brother finding us."

"We couldn't even catch who it was on our security cameras," Grayson said. "Our entire security system had been knocked out."

"We've had many threats and stalker trouble over the years," Bronwyn explained. "But they had never come near our home."

"The message had been written in a red substance that looked like blood." Grayson shuddered. "It wasn't. It was the fake blood used in movies."

"After that message, I had the tires slashed on my car when I'd taken my dogs to get their nails clipped," Bronwyn looked at Grayson. "Grayson got locked in the sauna at his country club."

"Those were the milder of the incidents that started after the break-in." Grayson looked at Bronwyn and pulled her hand into his lap. "We decided to make the trip when our children started being targeted."

"Why would someone be targeting you and your family?"

Ashley asked them. "And why do you think this company, Division Four, wanted you in exchange for Grace?"

"Division Four?" Grayson's eyes widened.

"Yes," Maria took over the conversation. "That company's name keeps coming up a lot around here lately."

"They were the ones sponsoring the big engagement party that my ex-husband and West's ex-wife were instructed to have at Cupids Bow ranch." Cat picked up the story from Maria. "They were the ones that hired a hit out of me, and David got shot." She looked around the room to find the man she loved. He was sitting quietly to one side, observing.

"They were the company that hired one of Cupid's Bow Ranch managers and his brother, Pete, the Double A ranch Forman, to steal livestock and kidnap Grace." David finished off for Cat.

"We think they are also the company that Winston Brown is working for, and they were probably behind the attempted kidnapping of Amy," Ryan told everyone.

"They were also the company that were trying to buy out my production company," Bronwyn told them.

"We think that Jason Brown owns Division four." All eyes turned to Ryan.

"I'm not sure how many of you have been told," Greg addressed the room once again, bringing all eyes back to him after the bomb shell Ryan had dropped. "But with some help, Tammy and her group managed to find out that the avalanche that took the lives of many including Tammy's brother, sister-in-law, and estranged husband was not a natural one."

"After a six-month-long investigation, the FBI has now concluded with the help of Wallace, Ashley, and their team, that the avalanche was set off purposely." Zac looked around the room.

The room fell into silent as all eyes were now waiting for Zac to continue.

"This is a timeline of events we've managed to put together

thanks to all of you submitting your findings to me," Zac said. "It begins thirty-seven years ago. Four weeks before our prom."

He turned and looked at Bronwyn, who nodded, and took over the conversation.

"I know many of you in this room, and I'm sure you all know me." Bronwyn looked around at the familiar faces. "I'm ashamed to say that I was the popular mean girl at school."

"I can attest to that," Tammy said, raising her hand before giving Bronwyn an encouraging smile.

"There's never an excuse for bullying anyone," Bronwyn told them. "No matter how dire your home situation is." She looked at Grayson, who took her hand in his for support. "I met and fell in love with Grayson during one of his visits to his father and brother in Lewistown."

"I lived in Billings because I have a heart condition, and all the treatment I needed was there," Grayson explained. "But I came home nearly every school holiday, for my birthday and other special occasions."

"That's why none of us knew you," Cat realized.

"Yes," Grayson nodded. "I was like a vampire. I couldn't go out in the heat of the day, and I had to be extra careful not to get any diseases until I got my heart transplant when I was sixteen."

"That's when we met." Bronwyn smiled up at him. "Greg and I always pretended to be in a relationship because he couldn't have the girl he wanted. I had a reputation to keep."

"Not many of you know this, but Bronwyn had Leukemia, which she fought hard to beat." Grayson shocked the room by saying. "I know there were a lot of other stories and rumors about her illness which made her miss a year of school. But she never wanted anyone to look at her with pity because she had cancer." He shrugged. "We understood each other." His eyes shone with love as he looked down at his wife.

"But cancer wasn't the only thing Bronwyn had to fight throughout her life." Greg took over for Bronwyn. "Bronwyn had a younger half-brother who came to live with them when he was eight, and he was quite a messed-up kid."

"He took after both my father and his crazy mother." Bronwyn's voice was tinged with anger and bitterness. "My father used to abuse my mother and loved to tell her how he only married her for her money. How he'd kept his relationship with the real woman he loved before they were married."

"I don't know how many of you met Bronwyn's father. But you'll remember how he always seemed to be such a nice guy." Greg's jaw clenched. "But at home, he'd drink and enjoy making sure his wife knew that there was nowhere she could run that he'd not find her. She was his source of income as he loved to call her."

"Greg was always there for me." Bronwyn turned and smiled at him. "No matter how terrible I was to others, he always saw the real me."

"We'd been friends for a long time." Greg pointed out. "Bronwyn's father even worked at the auction house for many years before her grandparents died and left their fortune to Bronwyn's mother."

"Thank goodness they had the foresight to safeguard my trust fund and my mother's money from him." Bronwyn shook her head. "My father always wanted a son, but when he had a daughter, I was ignored until he needed someone to abuse emotionally."

"Just after Bronwyn was born, her father found out that his girlfriend was having his son," Grayson picked up the story. "The man was so delighted and forced Bronwyn's mother to raise him as if she were her own."

"The man was a complete sociopath." Bronwyn spat. "Winston, my half-brother, grew up to be just like him, and became fixated on making my life a complete misery."

"It got really bad in Bronwyn's final high school year for both her and her mother," Greg explained. "Winston had grown a lot taller than Bronwyn's mother and had started to hit her."

"Four weeks before the prom my mother landed up in hospital. She had a broken nose, two cracked ribs, and a broken arm." Bronwyn's eyes misted up as she remembered that dreadful night. "Fearing to be alone in the house I took my mother, and we went and stayed at Greg's house. Grayson was home learning the family business."

"We managed to hide Bronwyn and her mother for two weeks until her father brought the police to our house." Grayson put his arm around his wife and pulled her close to him. "I landed up in jail for punching Winston."

"You dislocated the guy's jaw!" Greg reminded him. "Thankfully, Ashley's father is one of the greatest lawyers of all times and got the Browns to drop the charges against Wa..." He glanced at his brother whose eyes narrowed. "Grayson."

"That's when the feud between the Watsons and Brown men started." Grayson shook his head. "Everywhere Greg or I went in town Winston Brown and his friends would find us and cause trouble."

"Until one day they didn't realize my father and Ashley's father were with us." Greg looked at his brother. "We were coming out of Holly's café when Winston jumped Grayson. He swung a baseball bat at him, but Grayson jumped aside and hit my dad in the stomach."

"Winston told my dad that he was glad he hit him because of what he'd done to his father all those years ago." Grayson frowned. "Winston seemed to be under the impression that his dad had shares in my father's store and the auction house. He was convinced that my father had fired him and stolen his shares in the business."

"Just to be clear, my father never had shares in any business," Bronwyn made it clear. "He was a leach that latched on to whoever he could get as much of a free ride out of as he could."

"His family had disowned him when he was eighteen. He and his girlfriend had tried to run away and elope together." Grayson ran his hand through his head. "When he ran out of money he was forced to come back to Lewistown. His parents gave him an ultimatum that he either settle down with a decent wife or he'd never see a cent from them. When his parents died all their money went into Bronwyn's trust fund." He shook his head.

"You can imagine how well that went down with him. Especially as Winston had not been left anything and had never been acknowledge by his parents."

"Oh dear," Cat said. "I still don't understand why the Brown's and Watson's feud would impact all of us."

"We were all best friends having been on the football team together," Zac explained to Cat. "Soon it became a big rivalry thing between our group and Winston's."

"So, all this trouble and fear they've instilled in us for thirty-seven years is over some childish teenage boy rivalry?" Ashley looked at them aghast.

"No," Brett jumped into the conversation. "It is a lot more than that." He looked at the four people sitting next to him and then at West who nodded for him to continue. "There should be two more of us standing here today telling this story."

"But one of them was taken too young from a heart attack while the other became a victim of this sick revenge story. As did a lot of other of our loved ones," West picked up the story. "Like Maria's parents, Callum Sparrow, and Brian Anderson along with his wife."

"We don't want to lose anyone else," Brett looked over the faces staring at them. "We also want to assure you all that none of us had any idea until recently that our actions all those years ago had anything to do with all the trouble that has plagued our land over these three, nearly four decades."

"What suddenly made you realize it may have been your feud with the Browns?" Ashley asked them, leaning back in her seat and eyeing them carefully.

"I overheard you, Cat, Chelsea, and Maria in Maria's study that night of our first meeting when Brett was released from the hospital," Zac admitted. "You'd all somehow concluded that the trouble spanned from the night of our prom. You were also all irritated because you couldn't find any record of that night. All the evidence about it had vanished."

"Even the police records seemed to have been doctored about your accident." Maria looked accusingly at Brett. "Why did you never tell me you were badly injured from a car accident and not a football one?"

"I'm amazed that you bought that story, actually," Brett admitted to his sister. "Nan, Callum Sparrow, the Becketts, the Hitchins, Mr. Watson, and the Becketts all came together to protect us that night."

"Your father, Ashley, along with all of our parents, and the County Sherriff were the ones that made the night disappear," Zac looked at Ashley. "They had to for a few reasons."

"The first was to protect me and my mother," Bronwyn told them. "A few days before the prom my mother landed up in hospital once again with bruised ribs. Before my mother was released from hospital Dr. Debbie Hitchin pulled me aside when I went to fetch her. Bronwyn looked down at her hands, but everyone saw the tears welling up in her eyes. "It was the day before the prom." She lifted her eyes and wiped away a stray tear from her cheek. "She offered to help me, and mum get away from my father once and for all. I got hold of Grayson to ask him what I should do, and he brought his father in to help." Bronwyn wiped the rest of the tears away before continuing. "Before I knew what was going on, Mr. Watson had brought all his friends in to help." Her eyes ran over everyone in the room. "Those friends were the parents of most of you in this room."

"As they couldn't all go visit Bronwyn's mom, Dr. Debbie Hitchin, being her doctor, was the one who delivered their plan to her." Grayson continued the story.

"The plan to help Bronwyn and her mother escape was a simple but effective plan," Greg explained. "Dr. Debbie Hitchin delayed Bronwyn's mother's release from the hospital for another few days on the ruse there had been some complications and Mrs. Brown needed a few more tests."

"Ashley's father informed Bronwyn's father that there was to be an audit of Bronwyn's trust fund and his wife's estate, so all monetary transactions were frozen until further notice," Brett explained. "Of course, Mr. Brown was furious. He was too busy venting and trying to get to his wife's money to notice what was happening behind the scenes."

"Ashley's father had managed to get all Bronwyn's mothers and Bronwyn's money transferred to other trusts in new trust names," Grayson picked up the story from Brett. "He was the one with contacts able to relocate Bronwyn and her mother."

"The plan was for my mother and I to disappear on the night of the prom." Bronwyn bit her lip. "I was going to go the to the prom as normal, and Dr. Debbie Hitchin would smuggle my mother from the hospital while my father was occupied with being a chaperone at the dance. They were lending my mother the Hitchins van, which we would leave in Billings, where Grayson's mother would get us to LA." She looked lovingly up at Grayson. "Grayson was going to come with us to Billings."

"But things went wrong when Bronwyn's brother overheard Bronwyn and I taking on the phone earlier that evening," Grayson's voice was laced with anger. "As Bronwyn was about to leave for the prom, her father stopped her and locked her in her room. Mr. Brown also found out his wife was no longer in the hospital and started to connect the dots."

"Mr. Brown was furious and went to hunt down his wife." Greg's eyes darkened with anger. "By then Bronwyn had escaped through her bedroom window and headed to the prom."

"I got there just in time to be crowned queen," Bronwyn's eyes met Tammy's. "I'm so sorry Tammy for the way I walked past Greg, but I had to get his attention. I couldn't risk going to Grayson's place and getting caught again. I had to warn the parents that were helping my mother and me." She shook her head. "I also didn't want to get anyone else involved in my family's terrible mess."

"Mr. Brown hated most of our parents." Zac shook his head in disgust. "I can remember him always hounding my father to let him invest in our horse breeding program."

"I think he hounded most of our parents to get in on our various horse and livestock breeding programs and our beef supply," Brett told them.

"I was always so ashamed of my father." Bronwyn shuddered. "My mother hardly ever went out because she found it difficult to cover up her bruises."

"What happened on prom night?" Cat asked impatiently.

Bronwyn returned to the story of prom night. "All the parents were at the prom as chaperones, so no one would suspect them in aiding our getaway." She bit her lip nervously. "We didn't have cell phones in those days and the only way to warn the parents was to be there. But when I got to the prom, I saw Winston was there."

"That's when Bronwyn found me," Greg told them. "I wasn't aware of the plan at that point. Nor was I aware that Grayson had thrown a party at our place to make sure everyone who knew him would see him there, so they didn't think he'd helped Bronwyn."

"I told Greg everything," Bronwyn explained. "The next thing I knew, Greg had brought the help of his entire group of friends."

"That included me, West, Todd, Brian, and Brett," Zac gave Bronwyn and affectionate smile. "I managed to get word to Bronwyn's mother that the pickup point had changed because Winston had followed Bronwyn to the prom and that her husband was aware of the plans."

"Her father had gone to the Watsons' house, only to find a rip-roaring party and came face to face with Grayson instead of Mr. Watson." Brett took over. "West and I were at the Watsons' house when he arrived. The man pulled Grayson from the house, threatening to kill him if Mr. Watson didn't meet him within an hour bringing him back his wife and daughter."

"I didn't want to alert Mr. Brown to the fact that I knew about the plans to help Bron and her mother escape, so I let him take me hostage," Grayson explained. "It also allowed me to keep tabs on him and meant Brett and West could follow us to where he was taking me."

"It was no surprise when he took me to that alley near the hospital just off main street. It was where we were meeting up with Mrs. Hitchin and Mrs. Brown," Grayson told them. "But we weren't the only one's that had been taken there." He looked at Greg. "Winston had managed to stop Greg and Bronwyn from getting to the hospital by coming at Greg with a knife. Bronwyn tried to stop him, but he slashed her. That's when Greg jumped at him but Mr. Brown, with me in tow, came up behind Greg. He knocked Greg out before I could stop him."

# Chapter Eleven

# THE MEETING - PART 2

Brett remembered the incident well. "That's when myself and West stepped in." He looked at West. "West ran at Winston. He managed to disarm him and knock him out before scooping Greg up in a fireman's hold."

"When Mr. Brown was distracted, me and Brett managed to knock him out of the way," Grayson took over the story. "Mr. Brown tried to take a swing at me, as I ran past him and connected with my jaw."

"West started to topple backwards as the weight of Greg threw him off balance," Grayson told them. "That's when Todd, Zac, Brian, and Mrs. Brown arrived in the Hitchins' van."

"Mr. Brown was distracted by the sight of them long enough for me, Bronwyn, Grayson, and West, who was carrying and unconscious Greg, to get the van." Brett continued telling the group about the events that took place that evening. "Once we were all safely in the van and taking off, that's when Winston came around."

"We heard a blast coming from the alley way and saw that Winston had a gun," Zac jumped into the story. "The driver of the van panicked wanting to protect everyone inside it and took off too quickly in the wrong direction. They went forward instead of backward."

"The van just missed Mr. Brown who managed to jump out of the way," West told them. "When we started backing out of the alleyway Winston fired another shot that hit the van making the driver have to swerve as we heard another round being fired."

"That's when we connected with the pole and Mr. Brown who'd jumped in front of us trying to stop us from getting away," Grayson's voice dropped. "When the driver reversed again after seeing what they'd done they accidently sped backwards into the building wall behind us."

"You keep saying the driver," Ashley noted. "The report stated that Grayson had been behind the wheel that night of the crash."

"No, it was my mother," Bronwyn's admission had the entire room gasp. "She got so panicked when she'd seen Winston with that gun all she could think about was getting us out of that alley as fast as she could. She was trying to protect us."

"What happened when Mrs. Brown hit the building wall?" Tammy asked.

"West was sitting next to Mrs. Brown and hadn't had the time to put his safety belt on." Grayson looked at West. "He flew through the window upon impact." He shuddered. "Mrs. Brown was knocked unconscious. Even though I had been hurt, I knew that she couldn't be found at the wheel of that car. It wouldn't look good for her as we didn't know if Mr. Brown was even still alive."

"You swapped places with Bronwyn's mother?" Ashley looked at Grayson, stunned.

"Yes," Grayson admitted. "Winston had fled the scene when he heard police sirens. The coward didn't even stay behind to check if any of his family were hurt or even alive. I had just dragged Mrs. Brown out of the car when Dr. Debbie Hitchin arrived at the scene after trying to find us. I was trying hard to keep from blacking out so I could tell her the story, and she helped me move behind the wheel."

"Grayson!" Tammy breathed. "That was so stupid yet so gallant."

"That's when Dr. Hitchin phoned the café where she knew all of our parents were meeting," Zac told them. "Ashley's father went directly to the scene to do what he could. By then the police had arrived and Winston was nowhere to be seen."

"That's why all the records were spotty, and that night was erased," Cat said.

"Yes, our parents moved heaven and earth to cover up what had happened," Brett admitted. "Too many lines had been crossed that night, and all we were trying to do was save Bronwyn and her mother from two abusive relatives."

"Both Winston and Mr. Brown were given a deal they couldn't refuse. They would end up in jail unless they agreed to take it," Grayson told them. "They had no option but to comply. Mrs. Brown gave her husband and Winston the house and left them some money in an exchange for a divorce and him leaving them both alone."

"Mr. Brown's injuries were so bad they left him paralyzed." Zac rubbed his hand over his face. "Apparently, Winston's mother and her sister came back to town to look after them."

"Winnie Larson!" Cat, Ashley, and Chelsea said together.

"Yes, Winnie Larson," Zac confirmed.

"Mr. Brown died five months later," Brett told them. "We believe it was about six months after that Winnie and Callum Sparrow started dating. No one was aware that Winnie had been involved with Mr. Brown back then."

"That explains Winnie's hostility towards us then!" Cat piped up. "I never trusted her."

"If Winston is Winnie's son, who would make him Harris Conway's cousin," Chelsea deduced. "So that is how Harris and Winnie connect to all this."

"Not only that," Zac looked at Chelsea, "But Winnie's sister dated my father when they were in high school. She thought that Harris was my father's son."

"Or she was trying to make it seem that way because I think

she found out that Cupids Bow could only ever be owned by a Sparrow," Cat realized. "That's why Harris' paternity test was done after Winnie married my father."

"She was determined to get her hands on our land." Zac nodded. "But she didn't, and dad told Uncle Rupert, Ashley's father, that he'd found out who Winnie really was a few months before he died."

"That was why he wanted the divorce and to move all the trunks in the attic." Cat's eyes widened as she started to put it all together. Her hand automatically touched the pendant that could be outlined through her shirt. "He didn't want her to find the family heirloom or secrets the land hold."

"He also hid all the valuable information from the other five farms," Zac informed her. "Just in case anything else happened to those who were involved that night."

"Five farms?" Maria's brow crinkled into a frown.

"Yes, the Donaldsons' farm as well," Brett told his sister and turned to David.

"It turns out my grandfather was a direct descendant from one of the original families that traveled out here and started the ranches." David smiled at the shock on everyone's faces. "I found a letter my grandfather had written to me in which he explains everything. But that is digressing the main reason for this meeting."

"Do you know where Callum Sparrow hid all the stuff?" Maria asked.

"We have a hunch," Zac told her. "Brett, West, Greg, and I have already tried to get into the place where we figure my father hid all the stuff."

"And?" Ashley said.

"It seems to need some sort of key," Brett answered before Zac could.

Maria, Chelsea, and Ashley's heads turned toward Cat looking pointedly at the pendant she was still clutching through her shirt.

"What?" Cat looked at them, confused.

"What did your father tell you on your eighteenth birthday when he gave you your birthday present?" Ashley looked pointedly at the hidden pendant.

"Cat?" Zac frowned at his sister.

Cat sighed, glared at her friends for being traitors, and pulled the ruby pendant from beneath her shirt. There was a chorus of exclamations through the room once Cat held it up.

"You got mom's necklace!" Zac stared at the beautiful jewel.

"Dad gave it to me at my eighteenth birthday dinner," Cat told him. "I always wear it."

"What did dad tell you when he gave it to you?" Zac asked her.

"That one day, it would unlock our past, helping me understand the Sparrow, Hitchin, Parker, Anderson, Beckett, and Donaldson family place on the land. And also our responsibility to a land that had so much to give us," Cat repeated his words for the room to hear.

"That looks like the shape of the lock!" Brett walked closer. "Do you mind if we take a closer look at it?"

Cat reluctantly took the pendant from around her neck and handed it to Brett, who took it back to Zac, West, Greg, Grayson, and Bronwyn.

"It's more beautiful than I remember it to be," Zac said, mesmerized by the huge ruby.

"Is it real?" Grayson breathed.

"Yes, I can assure you it's real and probably comes from that big mountain that looms in the background, protecting us," Ryan told them.

"What do you mean?" Ashley was the first to ask the question.

"There are rumors that the mountain behind us contains a vein of very precious rubies such as this one." Ryan pointed to the gem in Brett's hand.

"Maybe that's why the Donaldsons and Browns want to get their hands on our land!" Maria guessed.

"If there are rubies like this in that mountain, Division Four, if it truly is them trying to take over our land, must know about them or the rumor." Ryan reached out to take a turn looking at the ruby. "It's magnificent."

"It fits the pattern of the key." Brett compared the gem to the pattern of the lock they'd found in the main cavern of the mountain that he'd sketched in the notebook he had with him.

"We need to try it," Zac said excitedly and looked at West. "We'll finally find all our family's treasures and secrets they once locked away in our attics."

"And maybe find out once and for all what the family feud is about?" West grinned.

"We'll all find what our family stashed away with Callum," Brett said. "But before we even attempt to go there again, I suggest we send our invisible enemy to jail."

"Of course," Zac agreed and returned to his timeline in his notebook. "It all fits the timeline. The first incidences on the ranches happened a few weeks after Mr. Brown died."

"They started to escalate right up until Winnie married Callum," Brett pointed out. "They started happening again around Cat's eighteenth birthday when we discovered Callum had started divorce procedures."

"That was around the time he cleared out Cupids Bow Ranch's attic and helped the rest of the ranches stow theirs away," Chelsea noted.

"My father died, and there was a spike in trouble again." Zac looked at the timeline on notepad carefully. "Cat and Maria left home not long after that. We get the letters that a developer wants to know what is happening about the offers he put in a year ago and sends new ones to each of us."

"What about my parents' plane crash? The police thought the plane had been sabotaged," Maria pointed out.

"The police suspected that my parents' airplane crash had something to do with the investigation they'd launched into the development company wanting to buy their land," Brett shared a bit of her parents' story.

"Was it my grandfather's development company?" David asked them.

"No, actually it was Division Four." Avery turned her tablet around for everyone to see. "I told you Division Four has been going for longer than Jason Brown was alive."

"We've tried to get information on the place," Wallace told Avery, "But there is a lot of red tape to go through."

"Luckily, I have quite high clearance, having worked with dangerous viruses since I started my internship." Avery grinned at the look on Wallace's face. "Due to escalating viral outbursts, I get top-level clearance to all the system databases." She typed on the screen. "I've got the information you need, and ... Oh, that's right. This guy."

"Which guy?" Cat gave Avery a curious look.

"The owner of Division Four is an Oswan Bjorn, but during dinner last night, Amy found out that Oswan Bjorn was an anagram for Jason Brown." Ryan's eyes shone with pride, and as hard as he tried, he couldn't keep that admiration for Amy from his voice.

"Or at least we suspect it is," Jude butted into the conversation. "The man spying on Amy is Winston Brown, also employed by Division Four."

"They were also the company my uncle sold his family's development company to," David told them. "I only found that out two days ago."

"So, everything points back to Division four, Jason Brown, Winston Brown, and Winnie Larson." Cat folded her arms across her chest. "I told you all that woman was up to no good."

"Yes, you did, numerous times." Maria gave Cat a cheeky smile.

"I still don't get what they are doing this is for..." Ashley looked at the people standing in front of them and glanced at Zac's timeline of major events.

"Revenge!" Amy, who'd not said much during the entire meeting, piped up. "There was trouble around the time Greg's father fired Mr. Brown, and I bet all your family supported his decision." She looked at everyone in the room that were now staring at her.

"Most likely, yes," Zac answered her honestly.

"It was obviously something that was started by Mr. Brown. He did petty things to get his money's worth from those he thought had wronged him." Amy once again had everyone staring at her in awe. "What? I've been listening while you've all been gabbing on." She shrugged. "My opinion is that Winston was the one who escalated the wrongdoing by actually getting physically violent and even pulling out a gun on the night of that prom." She bit her lip thoughtfully. "I think one thing everyone did wrong on that night was let Winston get away with what he'd done. He at least should have discreetly been sent to juvenile detention."

"Yes, you're right," Chelsea agreed with Amy. "In his mind, he'd managed to get away with what he did, and he thought he could do so again because it was covered up."

"Exactly." Amy nodded. "Then when his dad died and he could pin his death on the injuries caused by the accident, Winston started looking for a way to get revenge. To him, his father was someone he looked up to and followed. From what Bronwyn has mentioned, I take it Mr. Brown doted on Winston."

Bronwyn nodded in confirmation.

"When his dad died, he was left penniless and without his role model. His whole way of life changed when he had to live with a mother he barely knew, an aunt, and another male in the house." Chelsea continued forming a picture of Winston.

"Does anyone have any idea what Winston did after he graduated high school?" Amy looked at the people in the room.

"I think Winston inherited Division Four from his mother, Winnie Larson." Avery's brow knitted into a tight frown as she stared at her laptop. "I tracked Winnie Larson's movements once she left Cupids Bow. It seems she got married to Graham North, who was a textile mogul in Europe and the original owner of Division Four."

"She's like a black widow," Cat hissed. "What happened to Graham North?"

"He was almost eighty when Winnie married him, and according to articles, he was suffering from chronic heart disease." Avery read off her screen. "She took over the business and moved it into other lines of business, like construction." She looked up at David. "One of her first large acquisitions was Donaldson's Developments."

"Well, isn't that just peachy," David said through gritted teeth. "At least she didn't get Donaldson's Construction that my grandfather built up from scratch when he left the family development business."

"Oh, I'm sure she tried," Cat's voice filled with scorn.

"A few years ago, Division Four was bought by Oswan Bjorn who went on to expand the company further, dipping into many different sectors – including high-end technological developments," Avery read off her screen.

"Jason Brown must have bought it as his pseudonym so no one would associate it with him," Brett guessed.

"When my half-brother and his wife had Jason, he must've been brought him up swimming in a pool of red-hot anger and hate for all of our families," Bronwyn's voice was filled with sadness. "I'm so sorry my family has done this to all of you." Her eyes filled with tears.

"Oh, no, Bronwyn." Gwen assured her, compassionately. "Trust me, this is not your fault. You were as much of a victim as everyone in this room."

"What we have to do now is find a way to stop your half-brother and his son," Ashley suggested. "And if you look around you, you'll see that what they have done is brought everyone in this room closer together."

"Ashley's right," Cat agreed with her friend. "We're all home because of the circumstances your half-brother and nephew have created."

"See, I told you my friends always find the rainbow in the storm." Greg hugged Bronwyn. "Now, what do you think is the best way to trap your half-brother and nephew?" he looked at Bronwyn.

"You said they were after Grayson..." Bronwyn looked up at her husband. "And I think they wanted him because Winston hated him. He knew I was in love with Grayson. I bet he also wanted Grayson so he could get to me. So, let's use both of us to bait the hook."

"Sure, throw me to the sharks." Grayson threw up his hands. "While I'm not one hundred percent on board with being the chum to bloody your hunting waters, I really do not want you involved in this." He looked down at Bronwyn.

"Grayson, I owe everyone in this room for freeing my mother and me, even if it's indirectly." Bronwyn stood her ground. "I'm doing this with you."

"And I think I know just how we're going to do it!" Amy smiled mischievously when all eyes turned to her. "Who's up for a hike in the mountains?"

"Why in the mountains?" Ryan asked.

"Because if that gem really does come from the mountains surrounding your land," Amy pointed out, "I don't' think revenge is the only thing Jason and his father are after."

"But Jason is a millionaire boarding on a billionaire." Maria looked at Amy. "Do you really think he's so greedy that he wants to overflow his coffers with rubies as well?"

"Actually." Avery brought all the attention back to her. "His company is in trouble." She looked up, her eyes traveling over all the faces staring at her in shock. "I just managed to find their quarterly filings, and it is not looking good."

"Can I see those?" Brett walked behind Avery and looked down at her laptop screen. He scanned the pages and gave a low whistle. "Avery is right." He lifted his eyes. "Jason Brown is in trouble financially and with his investors."

"How was he going to acquire mine and Carlos Santiago's network studios for Ursula if he's in financial trouble?" Amy asked.

"I don't think he would buy them," Brett told her. "He was

either hoping to have you, Martin, and Carlos out of the way, or he intended to use Ursula to take the fall for everything."

"Oh, Amy," Avery gave her a warm smile. "Wallace managed to get statements from every doctor that said they wrote you a prescription and recanted their statements. They are going to lose their licenses but at least we can now get your name cleared. The scripts were always picked up by Ursula."

"I also managed to find out that your records at the rehab center were being falsified to keep you in there," Ryan told Amy.

"The facility management was being paid to ensure you stayed there and that information about your addiction was leaked to the press," Wallace told her.

"Tammy and I want to help get your reputation repaired," West smiled at her. "If you let us, we would like to help you get your name cleared. You will have the option to get your career back on track."

"That is if you no longer want to be retired from acting." Tammy leaned over and squeezed Amy's hand.

"I..." Amy's heart pounded in her chest. *Was it really that simple?* Then it dawned on her. While it had been confirmed that she was being drugged, she still didn't know if her brother had been involved in it. "Do you know if Martin was involved in having me drugged?" Her voice was soft and shaky.

"I have my top investigators trying to find that out for you, Amy," Wallace promised her. "As soon as I know, I will let you know."

"Thank you." Amy smiled.

She should be over the moon that there was evidence that she had been drugged to derail her shiny career. So why did her heart feel heavy? How come her soul wanted to run away to hide far from the spotlight?

"I'm so happy for you, Amy," Ryan's voice startled her.

She turned to find him sitting next to her on the sofa where Gwen had been before getting up.

"Thank you." Amy gave a small smile.

"There's still something bothering you, though, isn't there?"

Ryan's hazel eyes bore into hers like he was looking right into her soul.

"It's nothing." Amy shrugged. "I'm just tired after the very eventful night last night."

"I'm sure everyone here would understand if you wanted to go have a lie-down," Ryan assured her.

"Oh, no. Besides, I have to finish mapping out my plan to trap Winston and Jason." Amy forced herself to put on a brilliant smile.

It was what she called her plastic smile. The smile she'd always used when posing with her parents as the happiest little girl in the world. For the next hour, they discussed and molded Amy's plan into what they hoped would be the perfect operation to trap the Browns.

While everyone was deep in conversation and planning, no one noticed when Amy awkwardly stood and hobbled towards the kitchen. Once she got there, she found the back door open, and something compelled her to move toward it. Amy was about to step out into the yard when a movement caught her eye, and she froze. Her eyes met Goldie's, Avery's large red wolf. They stood staring warily at each other for a few seconds before Goldie made his way slowly and cautiously toward Amy until he was standing right in front of her. Not knowing what else to do, she carefully lifted her hand out to him. Even though her heart was pounding in her chest, she realized it was not from fear but exhilaration.

For some reason, Amy didn't fear Goldie, and oddly enough, she felt strangely connected to him. The big red wolf stuck out his head and sniffed at her fingertips before gently nuzzling them with his snout. Getting braver, Amy slowly reached out and slid her hand over the soft fur of his head. A feeling of peace and belonging swept through her at the first contact with his warmth. Amy gave a soft laugh when Goldie stepped slightly closer to her, letting her rub his ears almost like a cat would do. But then something startled him, and he sprinted off before she could stop him. He disappeared into the trees that surrounded the small river to the side of the house. Amy was left feeling alone and empty for a few moments until she realized who had scared the wolf off.

"Are you okay?" Ryan's deep voice zinged through her like an electric shock. "What were you thinking getting so close to that wolf?"

Amy turned her head to look up at him, expecting to see anger in his eyes. Instead, there was only understanding. She frowned, confused at the contradiction between his words and actions.

"I, too, bonded with a red wolf," Ryan confided in her. "Two, in fact." He smiled at the look of amazement in her eyes. "Only my mother knows about this, but when I was fifteen, I came across this young female wolf trapped in a snare." He shuddered. "I know this sounds bizarre, but when I was hiking through the woods, I had an almost overwhelming urge to suddenly change the way I was going as if something had compelled me to do so. I just had this feeling that I had to go that way."

"It doesn't sound bizarre at all," Amy watched him as he told her the story.

"The closer I got to where she was caught, the more anxious I became. It was like I had to be somewhere, but I didn't know where or why." Ryan gave a soft laugh. "I was so startled and relieved when I eventually found her. Then when my eyes met the blue ones of that big red wolf, I felt no fear. Only anger over the fact that some brute had set a trap to catch either her or some other unsuspecting wild animal."

"What did you do?" Amy stood staring up at him, caught up in with him in his moment.

"Without a second thought, I released her from the trap," Ryan rubbed the back of his neck. "Luckily, she was not too injured, nor had she tried to chew off her own foot yet."

"They really do that?" Amy's eyes widened incredulously.

"I believe so." Ryan nodded. "When I got home, I told my mother what had happened, and she'd told me that I had done a brave but foolish thing. She also said that if I had felt so compelled to follow my inner voice where it led me, that wolf and I must have some sort of spiritual bond."

"That's beautiful." Amy sighed. "Your mother sounds like she was an amazing woman."

"She was." Ryan smiled down at Amy.

"What happened to the wolf?" Amy asked him, not wanting to let go of this magical moment they were sharing.

"I saw her many times after that." Ryan looked into the woods to where Goldie had disappeared. "I always felt she was there in the shadows watching over me."

"What a wonderful story." Amy stared up at him, feeling drawn in by his hazel eyes.

"That night, when I fell asleep, I had a dream much like the one you had last night," Ryan shocked her by saying. "I was walking down a path with the very wolf I'd saved that day. As we walked, I heard her telling me about the choices I would have to one day make." He laughed again. "The last time I dreamt about her, she told me that setting something free wasn't always the answer because sometimes those you are trying to set free have actually come home."

"That was strange." Amy frowned.

"I know," Ryan agreed with her.

"What did your mother say about the dream?" Amy looked up at him curiously.

"I couldn't ask her because I had the dream the night before I found you on my bridge." Ryan grinned at the look of surprise in her eyes. "Would you like me to take you to your room to rest?"

"If the meeting has finished, I would rather go for a ride," Amy answered truthfully. "I'm feeling tired of being cooped up inside all day."

"I tell you what," Ryan said. "I'll go ask Avery if it is okay for me to take you for a ride, and I will show you some of the ranch. We can take my brother's horse, Villain. You will like him, and he is far better suited for two riders than Daisy."

144

"I have to ask," Amy looked into his eyes. "Why is your horse's name Daisy?"

"Because she is a blue roan, and if you look closely at her markings, they resemble blue daisies," Ryan told her. "I found Daisy at an auction a few months after my mother passed away. She was deemed unrideable. But the minute we saw each other, there was a weird bond between us." His eyes darkened with emotion. "When I saw her markings and coloring, I knew she was meant for me – a final gift from my mother, letting me know she was always with me." He cleared his throat. "You see, blue daisies were my mother's favorite flowers."

Instant tears sprung into Amy's eyes, and goosebumps tingled up her arms as a cool breeze wafted over her. She suppressed a shiver and swiped at a stray tear that managed to push its way over her eyelid.

"That's such a sad and beautiful story," Amy's voice was hoarse with emotion, and she had a sudden urge to wrap her arms around his waist and hold him close to her.

"So, this is where the two of you snuck off too?" Avery's voice had them both spinning around guiltily.

"Should you be standing on that ankle?" Liam asked.

Liam was standing next to Avery, and Amy could've sworn they'd been holding hands, but they had let go as soon as Ryan had turned around. Amy felt Ryan's shoulders stiffen beside her, and a glance at his face showed his eyes narrowing in on Liam. Amy was sure he'd seen what she had between Avery and Liam.

"And what are the two of you doing sneaking off our meeting?" Ryan's voice was low and dripping with suspicion.

"We came to get some air," Avery said quickly. "We also needed some young people's time." She gave Ryan a smug smile. "I'm sure you didn't notice too much, but the room is filled with a different generation to ours."

"Nice!" Ryan nodded and lifted his eyebrow. "And does your mother know about the two of you?" He counter attacked her, going straight in for the kill as Amy noted.

"What about the two of us?" Avery stood her ground.

"If you're going to sneak around and have a secret relationship, try unlinking your hands before you speak to someone you
don't want to find out about it," Ryan suggested.

"Ryan!" Gwen's voice snapped through the air like a whip.
"Leave them alone." She stepped up next to her daughter and
then put her arm around Avery's shoulders and hugged her. "Of
course, Maria and I know about the two of them even though
they don't know we do."

Amy watched Avery's and Liam's cheeks go blood red.

"And we couldn't be happier for them!" Maria walked into the
kitchen to join them.

"Mom!" Liam groaned and looked at Avery with a caged-
animal type look.

"This way." Ryan sighed and stepped into the kitchen to act
as a buffer so his niece and Liam could escape their mothers.
"Why do mothers and older sisters have to always be so embar-
rassing?"

"Because we love you." Gwen laughed and pinched his
cheeks before kissing them.

"You let them get away!" Cat Sparrow sounded disappointed
as she rushed into the kitchen. "I thought we would catch them
out this time for sure."

"Good grief!" Ryan rolled his eyes and then turned to Amy.
"You know what, let's just get out of here."

Amy nodded, laughing when Ryan bent down and scooped
her up because she couldn't run with him. As he rushed towards
the stables, Amy heard the three women's 'awing' at them.

# Chapter Twelve

# NOT EVERYTHING GOES ACCORDING TO PLAN

Ryan carried Amy into the stable, where they once again came across Avery and Liam. This time, they were standing, talking, and looking into a stall.

"Thank you for saving us, Uncle Ryan." Avery looked over at them as they drew closer.

"Sure," was all Ryan said.

Amy could feel he was still slightly unsure about the Avery and Liam dynamic.

"Fern is doing a lot better," Avery told Ryan, immediately grabbing his attention. "I think she will carry this foal to term this time."

Ryan put Amy down gently when they reached the stall of a Paint Quarter horse with a deep shiny dark bay coat splashed with the cleanest white markings. Her mane was dark with white weavings, as was her long tail. Her belly was wide with the foal, and she stood drinking water from her trough.

"She's beautiful," Amy breathed.

"She has not been well," Avery explained to Amy. "The last time she was pregnant, she lost the foal and went into a deep depression."

"Avery and Zac's daughter, Jamie, found an orphaned young foal for her." Ryan looked into the stable. "At first, we didn't think she was going adopt it. She just completely ignored the poor little thing."

"After an hour of her not letting me feed it myself, Jamie was about to take him away to hand feed him when Fern surprised us by eventually helping him," Avery smiled at the beautiful horse. "After that, Fern wouldn't let him out of her sight. She became quite a fiercely protective mother."

"She still is, even now that he's almost four years old." Ryan laughed. "Come and meet him."

"Uncle Ryan, you know Amy shouldn't be on her foot!" Avery shook her head at him.

"It's okay. I need to walk," Amy told her.

"Just don't overdo it," Liam advised and held out his hand to help her.

Amy accepted his help. They followed Ryan and Avery out the back of the stables and to one of the pastures, where one of the most beautiful horses that Amy had ever seen stood watching them from a few feet away.

Ryan had stopped at a table on his way out of the stable and taken some fruit from one of the containers. He climbed onto the fence and held a slice of apple out in his hand. The beautiful horse with its silky silver coat stood watching him uninterestedly until Ryan whistled for him and put another piece of apple into his hand. The horse ambled his way over to them, playfully knocked Ryan's head with his nose, then whinnied as if he was laughing.

"You're such a clown." Avery laughed at the horse that was even more beautiful up close and a lot taller than he looked standing off in the field.

"How big is he?" Amy asked, looking up at the animal.

"He's almost seventeen hands high," Liam told her.

"Amy, meet Diamond," Ryan introduced them. "This is Fern's adopted son."

"He is gorgeous," Amy breathed, staring at the horse. "What type of horse is he?"

"He is an Akhal Teke," Avery told her. "His mother died on the trip where a horse breeder was importing them."

Amy was surprised by the anger in Avery's voice.

"The people bringing the horse over didn't know what they were doing," Ryan explained. "As a result, the horses were all confiscated and the person who'd paid a hefty price for the horses took a huge loss when the female died."

"Diamond would've died too if Jamie hadn't been told about him." Avery's eyes gentled, and so did her voice when she reached up to pat Diamond. "Hello, my beautiful boy."

Diamond responded to Avery by hugging her with his neck and making her laugh.

"He loves Avery and Jamie," Ryan told her. "He is also a complete mommy's boy."

"When will you be able to ride him?" Amy asked Ryan.

"He's just turned four, so in about six months." Ryan put the apple slices on the fence, and Diamond immediately turned away from Avery to get them.

"So fickle!" Avery patted his neck as he happily munched on the apple slices before knocking at Ryan's arm for more.

"I don't have any more apples." Ryan shook his head at Diamond, who clearly didn't believe him. "Okay!" He laughed and pulled out two more pieces from his pocket. "Here you go." He put them on the fence once again.

"Why doesn't he take them from your hand?" Amy watched Diamond basically suck up the apple pieces.

"He will only eat out of either Avery's or Jamie's hand." Ryan put the last two pieces of apple he had on the fence before turning to Avery. "I'm going to take Amy for a ride on Villain and show her some of the ranch."

"Cool, can we come with?" Avery asked him.

"Of course," Amy said.

"I'll go saddle up the horses," Ryan said. "Are you okay waiting here?"

She nodded.

"Liam, will you stay with Amy? I'll saddle up Spark for you,"

Avery looked at Liam questioningly.

"Sure," Liam nodded. "I'm a huge fan of yours." He admitted when Avery and Ryan had left. "I was sorry to hear you were retiring."

"I didn't have much choice in the matter." Amy gave him a tight smile.

"Do you think you'll go back to acting when Tammy and West get the truth about what happened to you out to the world?" Liam asked her.

"I honestly don't know," Amy didn't know why but she turned to look at the stables. She could see Ryan saddling up a dark bay quarter horse.

"Even though it would be a terrible loss to the entertainment world," Liam told her, "You must always follow your heart, and if you decide to stay, I know my aunt Cat would love to have you help her with the studio she's opening up for local talent of all ages."

"That sounds amazing," Amy said. "For the record, I think you and Avery are well suited."

"Thank you." Liam smiled. "I've been telling her that for years until she finally came around."

"She comes from the most wonderful people, as do you." Amy smiled up at him. "But I think you should go and help those two because if I'm not mistaken, your mother and aunt are about to descend on you."

Amy pointed at Maria, Gwen, Cat, and Wallace, who were walking toward the barn.

"Good grief!" Liam rolled his eyes. "Excuse me." He dashed off into the barn.

A soft wet nose nudged Amy, making her laugh. She turned around to pat Diamond when a gloved hand covered her mouth and nose stifled her scream. Diamond whinnied loudly and reared up, stomping hard onto the ground. Amy started to wriggle and tried to scream once again, but her small frame was no match for the tall solid one that held her as if she was lighter than a feather.

The man whisked Amy silently away into the thicket of trees that adorned the one side of the ranch. Even though she knew it was futile, Amy still tried to struggle free of the man that had brazenly kidnapped her in plain sight. As he turned to squeeze them between two trees, Amy caught a glimpse of the paddock where Diamond was. To her amazement, the horse was hurtling towards the fence that neared the woods, clearing it with ease. Diamond's ears were flat against his head, and his thundering hooves caught her kidnapper's attention, making him turn.

"What the devil," he hissed.

The man quickly ducked between the trees, skillfully disappearing through them. He picked up his pace when the trees cleared a little and weren't so thick. While he ran, he spun Amy around and flipped her over his shoulder like a sack of potatoes. Amy hadn't been able to see his face as it was covered by a balaclava, but her new position had freed her mouth as well as her hands. She immediately started to scream, kick her legs, and hammer his beefy back with her small hands. Amy knew she was in danger of being dropped if he stumbled, but she didn't care. Her fight-or-flight reaction had kicked in, pumping adrenalin through her system, fueling the burning embers of anger she had been trying to suppress for far too long.

Soon, her fear was replaced by red hot anger and Amy fought harder against her kidnapper who nearly threw her flying when he came to a skidding halt. That's when Amy heard the low, angry growl, and she knew instantly, without having to look, it was Goldie.

"You again!" The man said through gritted teeth. "I was hoping to run into you."

Amy managed to turn enough to see him lift his bandaged arm. "You did this to me, you filthy beast," the man sneered, and Amy felt his hand move and reach into his jacket. "But this time, I came prepared." He gave a cruel laugh. "Your coat will make a great rug for my floor."

"No!" Amy started to struggle once again.

"Stay still," the man warned her. "My son said to bring you to him, and as long as you are still breathing, he doesn't care what condition you're in." He warned her as he pulled a lethal-looking knife that Crocodile Dundee would've salivated over out of his jacket.

"Please, don't hurt him," Amy tried to reason with the man. "Goldie, go away, shoo!" Amy tried to twist around to scare Goldie off, but the wolf ignored her and faced down the brute hanging onto her.

"Come on, Goldie," the man emphasized the name to torment her and tease the wolf, whose growls were getting more dangerous by the minute.

In a panic and fearing for Goldie, Amy dropped her upper body down, opened her mouth, and bit down hard into the solid muscle below the man's shoulder. She bit so hard her jaw ached, and she was sure she'd drawn blood. The man howled in pain and threw her off him onto the ground. As Amy landed with a winding thud onto the ground, her head struck an exposed root making her see stars. She watched Goldie lunge at the man through her blurred vision and the searing pain in her back. The wolf went straight for the arm holding the vicious-looking knife.

The man screamed and tried to throw Goldie off, but the wolf held on, and he lost the grip on the knife. It dropped out of his hand and sunk into Amy's hip as she tried to move out of the way. But her head was foggy and throbbing in pain. Amy knew she had to fight the blackness threatening to pull her under. Trying not to pass out or get sick, Amy pulled the knife from her hip and pushed herself to her feet. As she did, she saw the man manage to throw Goldie off him, and he lunged for the knife in Amy's hand, but she turned and threw it as hard as she could into the trees.

"You stupid woman!" The man screamed at her.

He started to run after the knife, but before he could, Diamond broke through the trees, rearing up in front of the man and knocking him against a tree. He hit his head and crumpled to the ground. Amy turned to look for Goldie, and her heart sank when she saw him struggling to get up after being flung off the man. She forced herself to hobble over to him, dropping to her knees.

"Goldie, please get up, boy." Hot tears welled up in her eyes and spilled out over her cheeks. "Please get up." Without an ounce of fear, she pulled the wolf's head onto her lap, stroking his fur.

It didn't take too long, and Goldie managed to get up once he'd got his wind back. His ears twitched, and he went on alert, giving a soft growl in the direction the man was taking her.

"Dad!" A man's voice called at a lowered pitch through the trees.

Amy could hear the crunch of leaves as his heavy footstep drew nearer.

"Do you have her?" The man called.

"Dad?"

All the hairs on Goldie's back rose, and he jumped in front of Amy protectively. She sat there startled for a few minutes, hearing the man's steps grow nearer. Amy wasn't sure what to do as she didn't even know if she could get up. Her head still ached, and her vision was still a little blurry. Her ears were ringing, her hip burned, and her ankle throbbed. But Amy was not a quitter, and there was no way she would sit there waiting to be recaptured. Especially after Goldie and Diamond had come to save her.

Her head turned to see Diamond start to stamp on the ground as he shook his majestic head while Goldie stood guard over her. Amy knew she had to get away, but there was no way she would outrun anyone in her condition. She glanced up at Diamond and knew there was only one option which was even more dangerous than being recaptured, but she had to try. Amy managed to stand up and hobble over to Diamond, who instantly settled the moment she touched his side. She wasn't sure she had the strength to pull herself up onto the tall horse's back or if he'd even seat her. Diamond had never been ridden and had only just turned four.

"I'm so sorry, boy," Amy whispered to him. "But you're my

only hope right now as Goldie might be big, but there is no way I can ride him out of here."

Diamond stood completely still as if he'd understood what she said. Amy put one hand on his withers and used all the strength in her upper body and her good leg to push and pull herself up onto his back. To her surprise, other than a slight movement, Diamond stood patiently, letting her flop onto his back and clumsily switch herself into a sitting position. She tangled her hands in his mane when none other than Jason Brown stepped into the clearing.

His startled eyes met Amy's, but before he could react, he jumped back when Goldie sprang forward, growling warningly before he saw his father lying unconscious on the ground.

"Dad!" Jason shouted.

As soon as he was distracted, Amy kicked Diamond into action and called for Goldie to follow them. Amy gripped Diamond's mane as tight as she could as the young horse rushed forward straight toward Jason, who jumped aside. Amy flew past him with Goldie right by their side, disappearing further into the woods as they fled from her kidnappers. Amy, Diamond, and Goldie sped through the trees until they finally came to an opening. Amy didn't know where they were or how long she'd been riding. Her head was pounding when she managed to slow Diamond to a trot, not knowing how much longer she could hold onto him. The world around her seemed to be throbbing in the rhythm of the pain torturing her entire body. All she wanted to do was lie down for a little while and rest. She was getting so tired. Amy brought Diamond to a halt and managed to slide off his back.

"You're a good boy," Amy leaned against him as she weakly ran her hand down his sweaty neck. "Oh no!"

She tried to see just how hard she'd ridden him. But the world around her started to spin. Amy knew she couldn't lie down where she was; it was too open. With the last bit of strength and will she had left, Amy dragged herself over to the cover of some trees. She just had to sit down for a few minutes, and then she would walk Diamond back home.

A soft whine drew her attention, and Goldie sild towards her, curling up next to her.

"Thank you, my friend," Amy said. Even speaking was starting to become tiring. "I'm just going to sleep for a few minutes."

She rested her head back against the tree. Her eyes slid shut as Amy let the world disappear into the sanctuary of darkness that dulled the pain searing through her.

"*R*yan!" Wallace's panicked call immediately had him on high alert.

"Amy!" Liam yelled, stopping on his way into the stables and twisting around to disappear back out of them again.

Ryan knew instantly that Amy was in trouble. He dropped everything in his hands and sprinted in the direction he'd seen Liam go.

"Diamond!" Ryan heard Avery scream, but he ignored her cries as he saw a hooded figure disappear into the east woods of his property.

"Ryan, Liam," Wallace barked out the command. "Wait!"

Ryan ignored Wallace and was about to dash past Liam when Wallace shouted, "Liam, stop him."

Liam turned, dive-tackled Ryan, and then rolled them out of the way as he saw Diamond fly over the fence and soar above them.

"What the..." Ryan pushed Liam off him and stared in shock at Diamond as the horse galloped into the trees after the man who Ryan knew had Amy.

Ryan immediately sprung to his feet and was about to follow the horse when Wallace's hand clamped around him, stopping him.

"Think wisely about this," Wallace hissed in Ryan's ear. "We do not know how many men they may have in those woods, and you are no use to her dead."

"Right now, he is gaining ground, and standing here cowering over a few men that may or may not be hiding in the wood is costing us time!" Ryan yanked himself out of Wallace's grip.

"Zac and the rest of the men are on their way," Wallace told him. "They are bringing weapons, and the Sherriff's department is also on their way."

"We were coming to tell you that one of the ex-ranch hands working for Division Four flipped on Jason Brown." Gwen caught up with them. "Once that guy did, it wasn't long before all the other men working for him flipped to cut deals."

"The FBI and every law enforcement agency are on the lookout for Jason and his father, who are on the run," Maria said.

"Right now, all I'm worried about is finding Amy," Ryan looked over as Zac, Brett, Greg, Jude, Grayson, West, and David ran towards them.

"We know the area much better than they do," Zac pointed out. "Let's split into groups of two and take a section of the ranch each."

"I'll go in the direction the man who has Amy, and my horse went," Ryan said, looking over at Greg. "Greg, will you come with me?"

"Definitely." Greg stepped forward as Zac handed Ryan a weapon.

"We'll keep in touch on our phones," Zac said.

Before he could finish talking, Ryan and Greg set off in the direction the man had taken Amy while the rest of the men paired off, taking the sections of the ranch Zac delegated to them. Ryan and Greg slipped into the woods, tracking the man through the trees. Luckily for Ryan, whoever had taken Amy was not as skilled as they had thought when he'd broken into their house the night before. He hadn't covered his tracks at all.

They hadn't gone too far when they heard Amy start to shout and call for help. Ryan and Greg looked at each then sprang into action. They silently pushed forward, following Amy's voice, but stopped when her shouting ceased. A terrible growl ripped through the woods, they heard Amy shout, "No!" and then everything fell silent once again. They carried on straight ahead in the direction they'd last heard Amy's voice coming from until the man's agonizing scream split the silence. Once again, Greg and Ryan looked at each before picking up their pace and rushing toward the shouts.

As Ryan and Greg came to the clearing, they watched in horror as a blood-stained Diamond with Amy clinging to his back flew off in the opposite direction,

"Is that a wolf running next to them?" Greg's eyes widened.

"Yes," Ryan said, but he didn't have time to explain before Jason Brown saw them.

Jason's eyes widened in shock. He spun around and started to run from them.

"I'll handle Jason and his father!" Greg hissed, his eyes darkening dangerously. "You go after Amy."

Ryan nodded and took off after Amy. He didn't want to lose ground or time but knew it would take him much longer to find her on foot. Ryan didn't stop running after them as he pulled out his phone and called Wallace to tell him they'd found the Browns. As he ran, he told Wallace he was leaving a trail and asked him to bring Villain for him.

Ryan didn't know how long he'd been running when he heard the sound of horses gaining on him. He turned to see Wallace riding towards him with Villain in tow.

"Greg told me he thinks Amy is badly injured," Wallace said, slowing down.

Ryan didn't waste a moment as he mounted Villain. "There was a lot of blood on Diamond's side, but I'm not yet sure whose blood it might be."

Ryan took off at a gallop with Wallace right by his side as they followed the fresh, unique trail left behind by a horse with a wolf running beside it.

"Are those wolf tracks?" Wallace called as they thundered along next to the prints.

"Yes," Ryan answered, not taking his eyes from the path leading them to Amy.

"Ryan!" Wallace called, turning his horse when the tracks suddenly stopped. "Over there."

Ryan turned Villain toward the direction Wallace was pointing. His heart stopped when he saw Diamond standing and grazing near a tree without a rider.

"You were right," Wallace said softly. "That is a lot of blood on Diamond's side."

Ryan slid off Villain and handed the reins to Wallace, "Can you stay here and hold Villain?"

"What if you need help?" Wallace took the reins.

"I will signal you," Ryan told him. "If Amy is there, she may be with a big red wolf who's seemed to have made himself her protector."

"Ah, like Avery's Big Red all those years ago?" Wallace remembered the story Ryan had told him about the wolf.

"Yes, except Goldie is a little bigger than his father and seems to be much more protective," Ryan warned Wallace.

Ryan had to stop himself from rushing over to where he saw Diamond's ears flicker and his head turn towards him. Ryan spoke softly and gently as he approached the tree where the horse was standing. As he got closer, Ryan froze when she heard a low growl. His heart started to pick up speed when he saw Goldie, who had positioned himself protectively over Amy. Flashes of another time sped through his mind – back when his twelve-year-old niece had gone missing in the mountains.

Ryan's eyes took in all the blood on Goldie's coat, and his heart lurched even more.

"It's okay, boy," Ryan said softly. "I'm not here to hurt her." His eyes roamed over Amy's still body lying curled up on the ground at the foot of the tree. "Please, Goldie, I need to get to her."

Goldie slid forward with his teeth bared, and as he did Ryan's blood turned cold when he saw the bloodstain beneath Amy. His eyes narrowed angrily on the big wolf. Ryan didn't have time to talk the animal down. He needed to get to Amy. He was about to try and knock the wolf off her when he heard Avery's soft voice from behind him.

"Hey, boy," Avery moved to crouch down beside Ryan. "Uncle Ryan, back away," she said beneath her breath. "Goldie is not like Big Red."

"He'd better not have hurt her!" Ryan said through clenched teeth.

"He wouldn't," Avery assured him. "Please, Uncle Ryan, back away. I can both handle Goldie and help Amy."

"I'm not going far," Ryan told her stubbornly.

"We don't have time for your stubbornness," Avery hissed as she eyed the blood on the ground. "Go!"

Ryan reluctantly backed away but stood near enough to pounce if Avery or Amy needed him.

"Ryan, help me with Diamond," Gwen put a gentle hand on his shoulder. "We'll have to get him into a horse box."

"I'm staying here," Ryan didn't take his eyes off Avery as she managed to get Goldie to let her get near Amy.

While Avery examined Amy, Goldie moved into the cover of the trees as more cars pulled up, including two emergency vehicles and a helicopter.

"Uncle Ryan," Avery turned towards him and called. "Please, I need you and Wallace to keep Goldie back so the medics can get Amy."

The next few minutes seemed like torturous hours to Ryan while Avery worked with the medics to get Amy into the helicopter. He stood by helplessly and watched, with no one telling him anything about her condition. All Liam could tell him was that she'd lost a lot of blood and that Ryan could ride with him to the hospital if he wanted to. Ryan didn't even remember answering him but found himself on the way to the hospital in Liam's car.

# Chapter Thirteen

# THERE ARE MANY TYPES OF TREASURES

he next couple of hours went by in a blur of people coming and going around him. Ryan vaguely remembered someone telling him that the feds had Jason and his father – that they had found all the evidence they needed and that the Browns and Winnie Larson had been behind all the trouble. Winston had even confessed to being the one that had killed Callum Sparrow. He told the feds that his father had paid someone to tamper with the plane that had the Parkers killed.

Ryan knew that he should be feeling relieved that all the trouble was finally over, but instead, all he could think about was the wasted lives and Amy. He'd had a fan's crush on her since he'd been in high school like millions of other guys around the world. Never in a million years would Ryan think he'd ever get to actually meet her. He'd met her once before at Tammy and her brother's wedding. Amy had barely looked at him back then when she breezed into the reception on the arm of some hotshot actor.

His niece was also a huge fan of Amy's, and she kept him well informed about Amy's life. When he'd met her after she first arrived in Montana with Tammy Anderson, it had been a shock to see her as a real person and not some sort of untouchable idol. The more he ran into her and got to her know over these past weeks, the more he begrudgingly found himself liking her. She was either the best actress in the world, or she was not like the tabloids and the media made her out to be at all.

Ryan had done his best to see her as a spoiled, pampered city girl, but she'd somehow gotten past the barriers he'd erected and wiggled her way into his heart. It had been a shock when she'd told him about her dream and an even bigger one to see her wolf seek her out. His mother always told him that the wolf would also guide his true soul just like he was. Because a wolf, like the horse, saw your soul; they were able to see the kindred spirit's soulmate and would guide them both home to each other.

"Ryan, I got you a cup of coffee," Tammy's voice broke through his thoughts.

"Thanks." Ryan took the steaming cup of coffee Tammy handed him. "How long is this going to take?"

Tammy sat down next to him with a cup of coffee in her hands, "I think the doctors and nurses are sick of me asking them if there's an update every few minutes."

"They're lucky it's you and not Ryan," Gwen said as she and Jude walked into the waiting room Ryan and Tammy had been ushered into when they'd arrived at the hospital.

"I believe Liam is in surgery, and Avery is watching from the student observation room," Jude told them.

"Ryan and I just want to know why this is taking so long." Tammy put her coffee cup on the table in front of her. "We've been waiting here for almost two hours."

"We needed to do a thorough examination of Amy as she wasn't conscious to tell us where she was hurting!" Avery had come into the room so silently that she made them all jump.

"Is she going to be okay?" Tammy and Ryan said together.

"She lost a lot of blood," Avery told them. "But we managed to stabilize her and get all the debris from the wound on her hip." She looked at Ryan. "Do you have any idea how she injured her hip?"

"No," Ryan shook his head. "By the time Greg and I got into

the clearing where Winston, Amy, and Jason were, she had flown off on Diamond's back."

"We think it's a knife wound. It needed fifteen stitches. It was what accounted for Amy's blood loss." Tammy eyed the coffee Ryan put on the table in front of him. "She has a bad bump on the back of her head that needed stitches too."

"We found evidence of some sort of scuffle where we found Winston and Jason," Jude informed Ryan. "There was a lot of blood in the one spot where Amy must have fallen or been tossed to the ground."

"She has bad bruising on her back and a few ribs." Avery looked at Jude. "It must've been from that, and judging by her bruises, which must've been quite a fall she took. I'm surprised she managed to get up at all after that sort of impact."

"Amy is a fighter." Tammy smiled fondly. "The one thing she never does is give up."

"She is quite a tough little thing." Ryan gave a small laugh.

He remembered how she'd pulled herself up even when her foot must've been killing her when he'd found her just a few days ago.

"I've examined Winston Brown," Avery walked over to the table and picked up the cup without asking to take a sip. "Thanks," she said, adopting his cup of coffee. "He has a few sets of bite marks on him. Two fresh sets on his one arm and one that I think he got when he broke into Amy's room."

"That must've been that big red wolf you said saved Amy," Tammy looked at Ryan, who nodded.

"So, it was him!" Ryan's eyes flashed dangerously.

"Yes, he confessed to it," Jude looked at Ryan. "Actually, he bragged about it."

"The man is unhinged," Greg joined them, walking over to kiss Tammy before taking a seat next to her. "He also wants to sue all of us for our vicious animal attacking him."

"Is he serious?" Ryan stared at Greg in amazement.

"Yes, and he is rather confident that he's not going to be in prison for long," Greg told them. "Winston said, and I quote, I won't be in here for long, and when I'm out I won't be so subtle about taking the whole lot of you down – including my high and mighty sister."

"Nice." Tammy shook her head. "What is Jason saying?"

"He confessed to his part in it all only because his lawyers advised him to cooperate," Jude said. "According to Wallace, they probably won't ever see the light of day again. All Jason's assets have been frozen, and his company has been seized by the government."

"His grandmother couldn't be very happy." Gwen looked at Jude.

"Winnie Larson is in a care facility and has dementia," Jude informed them. "The FBI wants to move her to one of their secure facilities to keep an eye on her. One of the agents working the case is not convinced about Winnie's condition."

"I don't blame them for being cautious with that woman," Ryan said. "She was not a nice person and carried so much bitterness inside her."

"My heart aches for Cat and Zac." Gwen's eyes filled with emotion. "It must be both a relief to find out how Callum died and a pain to be reliving it all over again."

"Cat always thought that Winnie had something to do with Callum's death," Ryan told them. "To be honest, I thought so too."

"I remember!" Gwen looked at her brother and shook her head. "The four of you caused quite a stir over it."

"I remember that!" Tammy smiled at Ryan. "You, Cat, Chelsea, and Ashley were trying to get the police captain to investigate Callum's death."

"I'm still reeling from the fact that everything that happened was because of my family," Greg said, his voice full of regret. "I have no words and don't even know how to begin to fix this."

"Greg!" Tammy put her hand on his leg. "Mr. Brown had started this feud with our families' years before that night."

"Winston was only too happy to spill out the whole story of how his father tried to get back at your six families because he'd been wronged by them." Jude sat back and put his arm around the back of Gwen's chair. "After Mr. Brown died, Winnie Larson took up the man's grudge, except she was even more bitter and twisted than he was."

"Poor Jason really didn't stand a chance, having grown up with all that hate and bitterness," Avery Gwen said.

"At least they are all behind bars now," Avery butted into the conversation and looked at her wristwatch. "I have to go and check on Amy as she should be out of surgery by now." She looked at Ryan, "Oh, there was also a rather vicious bite mark on Winston's back." Avery couldn't hide her smile. "If I had to guess without taking an imprint of Amy's jaw to compare against it, I'd say that is how she freed herself."

"When can we see her?" Tammy asked before Ryan could.

"We're taking her to the ICU," Avery dreaded telling them this and thought she'd manage to escape before she had to.

"Why the ICU?" Ryan's eyes narrowed.

"It's just a precaution as the bump on her head caused a slight swelling in her brain," Avery told them.

"How slight a swelling?" Jude asked Avery through gritted teeth.

Ryan turned to look at him, and his face had paled.

"I will know more once she is out of surgery, which she should be around now." Avery looked at her wristwatch again, and before there were any more questions, her pager went off. "Sorry, I have to go." She took the last sip of coffee and plopped the cup back on the table.

"Is it Amy?" Ryan jumped to his feet

"Uncle Ryan, please, keep calm and wait here." Avery looked to Greg for help as she didn't think Jude, who was staring at her like a pale stone statue, would be of any help at that moment.

"Ryan," Greg stood up and blocked his path. "We're all worried about Amy, but you're not going to do her any good by going off all hot-headed."

While Greg talked Ryan down, Avery slipped out of the room, pulling the door behind her.

Ryan knew Greg was right, but still, he had to fight the urge to physically remove him from his path so he could rush after Avery to demand more information. He glanced at the closed door before sitting down next to Tammy once again.

"Should we go get some more coffee?" Tammy asked him.

Ryan was about to say no when he saw the sparkle in her eyes. Tammy also wanted to know more about Amy and going to get coffee was a way to sneak out to do so.

"Sure," Ryan stood up with her and looked around the room. "Does anyone want anything from the cafeteria?"

Tammy and Ryan took the orders, and as they left, Gwen joined them.

"You really didn't think anyone here was buying the 'go get refreshments with a detour to pound out some information from Amy's doctors' act, did you?"

Ryan and Tammy looked at each then glared at Gwen.

"Don't worry," Gwen whispered. "I'll cover you."

*I*t had been two weeks since Amy had been in the hospital. When she finally woke up, she'd been so confused and panicked to find her mind blank. Amy's eyes had flown around the room, and she got even more anxious when she realized she was in a hospital. That was until she felt a warm hand enfold hers, and she turned her head to look into a pair of familiar hazel eyes. Her heart skipped a beat as she remembered Ryan's soft words.

*"Hey, sleepyhead, you're finally awake!"*

That was all it took. Those six words filled all the blank spaces in her mind with her memories once again. Amy closed her eyes and took a deep breath. It was nearly two in the afternoon, and Ryan would be back to visit. He and all her other friends would visit her every day she'd been in the hospital. While Tammy, Gwen, and the others took turns to visit her every day, Ryan came morning, afternoon, and evening to see her.

In the evenings, he would read her a book his mother had read to him about the tales of a wolf.

Amy had been so surprised to find out that the book's author had been his great-grandmother. She had written a series called the Spirit Animal Souls. The one Ryan thought she'd be interested in was the one about the big red wolf. When Ryan had first started reading it to her, it had sent chills up her spine. The story could've been about her and Goldie; it was so eerily similar to hers. The door to her room opened, and Amy's heart lurched. She had to fight to keep the disappointment in her voice when she greeted Gwen.

"Hello, Amy," Gwen grinned. "You won't believe the news Tammy and West have for you," she said excitedly and popped her head out of the door. "They were right behind me."

Amy frowned as she craned her neck to see if Ryan was with her, but he wasn't. Instead, Tammy and West followed Gwen into her room.

"Amy, look!" Tammy hugged her before showing her the tablet Wes had in his hands. "The news about the avalanche, Ursula, and Jason Brown is finally out."

"And..." West leaned over Tammy, took the tablet, fiddled on it, then handed it back to her, "Watch."

A news bulletin flashed on the screen. It was about Ursula and Jason. They went on to speak about the terrible things they'd done to Carlos and Martin. When the news presenter had finished talking, he told the audience he was on a call to Montana. To Amy's surprise, West's face appeared on the screen, and he proceeded to tell the world about how Ursula had drugged Amy. After a few questions from the news presenter, West left the interview. The presenter went on to speak about the terrible wrong Amy Guest had been through.

"Your name has been cleared. You must see all the responses on the news site to the segment," Tammy told her excitedly. "West has been on the phone with so many TV shows that would like you to come on and tell your story."

"I've already had offers for two movies and a new television show for you." West grinned.

"That's awesome. Thank you both so much." Amy put on her best plastic smile while trying to hide an overwhelming urge to spring from the bed and flee for her life.

"Some more good news," Gwen stepped up to her. "Avery said you will be able to go home tomorrow."

"That is the best news." Amy breathed a sigh of relief. "Although I really wish I could go home today."

"Only one more night here." Tammy smiled. "I've already instructed Julia to get your room at Double A ready for you."

Amy couldn't help it. Her fake smile dropped as she heard that, and her eyes met Gwen's.

"Or you are more than welcome to come back to Four Lakes if you want to." Gwen gave her a warm smile. "It is your home now too."

Tammy looked a little hurt for a few seconds before recovering as she glanced at Gwen and then looked back down at Amy. "Of course, if you are more comfortable at Four Lakes, you have that option too."

"Tammy, you have been nothing but supportive to me when I've needed you the most," Amy told her. "But you've got a whole new life here in Montana now, and a few new extended family members." She saw Tammy laugh. "If you and Gwen don't mind, I would very much like to go back to Four Lakes."

As she said that, she heard a noise at the door. Her head moved, and her heart jumped in joy when she saw Ryan standing there with a big smile on his face.

"You do know that I'm going to hound you to make sure you're okay, though," Tammy warned her, taking Amy's hand.

"Tammy and I will continue making sure your reputation is restored," West promised. "Then when you are ready, we'll go over the shows and options you now have to restore your amazing career."

"Thank you." Amy looked at both of them.

"Do you mind if I interrupt?" Ryan decided to butt in at that moment. He had two large cups from a well-known coffee shop in his hands. "Sorry, I didn't realize you'd all be here today. I only bought two of these."

"It's okay," Tammy smiled down at Amy. "West and I have to get going anyway. We are helping Cat with her new studio. Greg, Brett, Wallace, and Jude are there too, giving their few cents worth of advice."

"We will see you tomorrow," West said his goodbyes and waited patiently for Tammy to do the same. "Gwen?"

"I'll be there in a minute," Gwen told him and then turned to Amy. "I'm very glad that you are coming back to stay with us." She leaned forward to say softly. "I know at least three people back at the ranch that miss you dearly." She winked as she stood up and left the room.

"I brought you one of those hot chocolates I told you about." Ryan walked into the room and put the cups on her nightstand. "I also brought you this." He handed her a brightly wrapped present.

Amy took it and pulled off the wrapping paper. To her surprise, it was the book he'd been reading her.

"Ryan, this is your family's copy," Amy looked at him wide-eyed.

"No, it's my copy, and I want you to have it." Ryan picked up one of the cups, slid a chair closer to the bed, and sat. "Each of us at Four Lakes had one, so we have a few of them lying around."

"Are you sure?" Amy's heart beat so fast at the thoughtful gift that she felt quite breathless.

"Yes." Ryan nodded. "Oh, I have another surprise for you." He grinned while taking a sip of his drink, and he turned toward the door to see a nurse coming in with a wheelchair. "I finally convinced Liam and Avery to let me take you out into the gardens to get some air."

"Can't I walk instead?" Amy eyed out the chair with distaste.

"Sorry, the only way they'd let me do this is if I initially pushed you out into the garden," Ryan explained.

"Fine," Amy relented, already swinging her legs over the bed. But to her surprise, they started to buckle when her feet touched the floor.

Ryan shot out of his chair and plopped his coffee down to catch her, but the nurse had already steadied her.

"You have to take it slow, Amy," the nurse advised her. "You've been lying in bed for just over two weeks now."

Ryan and the nurse helped Amy into the wheelchair. He handed her their cups of chocolate and pushed her through the halls and into the lovely garden out the back of the hospital.

"This is beautiful." Amy sighed, looking around her. "Do you think I could get up and try walking for a bit?" She looked up at Ryan.

"Sure, let's just go over here." Ryan pushed her to a bench with a table. Ryan took the cups and put them down before turning to her. "Do you want to try standing again?"

Ryan held out his hands to her, and Amy's stomach fluttered while her heart skipped a few beats when her small hands slid into his large warm ones. Ryan gently pulled her up. She stumbled as her jelly legs threatened to buckle again, but he caught her and pulled her to him.

"Careful does it." Ryan's voice rumbled through his chest, and his heart thudded against her ear. "I'll turn you around, but keep my hands on your waist," he instructed. "Is that okay?"

Amy didn't trust her voice, so she nodded as Ryan helped her turn.

"Let's try this again." Ryan was true to his word and kept his hands on her waist as Amy forced her jelly legs to work.

"It feels so good to stand and walk again," Amy told him. "I've felt like I was becoming a part of that darn hospital bed."

"I can imagine," Ryan gave a soft laugh. "I'm going to let you go now, okay?"

Ryan made sure she was steady before releasing his hands from her waist. Amy suddenly felt so cold that she nearly buckled but forced herself to remain steady. How would they let her go home tomorrow if she couldn't walk on her own?

Amy walked a few feet away from Ryan, enjoying the feel of stretching out her tight muscles. She turned and caught her breath at how Ryan looked at her with such emotion and pride.

"I can't wait for tomorrow," Amy said – or rather squeaked – and quickly cleared her throat.

"I bet!" That was all Ryan said as he watched her make her way carefully back to him. "So, you're coming back to Four Lakes," he said so matter-of-factly that Amy frowned.

"Oh, I'm so sorry," Amy suddenly realized that she'd not asked him if he was okay with her going back to his home. "I didn't even ask you if that was okay." Her eyes searched his. "Do you mind?"

Ryan stared at her intently for a few heart-stopping moments. Amy felt her heart start to plummet to her feet. She thought he was about to tell her he didn't want her there when he completely surprised her. Ryan took the two steps that were between them. He reached down, cupping her chin and tilting it toward him before plastering his lips to her in a soul-searing, heart-pounding kiss.

He finally lifted his head, leaving Amy dazed and a little giddy. Ryan didn't take his hands from her face, and his voice was hoarse with emotions as he said, "Does that answer your question?"

# Chapter Fourteen

# THERE ARE SOME STARS NOT MEANT TO BE REACHED

The following week went by in a blur as Amy got released from the hospital. Her stitches were all out, her bruises were slowly fading, her ribs were getting better, and her ankle was healed. She was feeling on top of the world as she soared across the fields on the back of Villain, laughing as she raced Ryan on Daisy to the Four Lakes property line. When she got to the spot, they'd been going to near the farthest river on the ranch, Amy was surprised to see a picnic set up beneath a tree.

She pulled Villain to a stop and swung him around as Ryan caught up with her.

"I beat you again." Amy grinned at him. "Did you set out a picnic?"

"No, I had one of the ranch hands do it," Ryan said as he slid off Daisy and then helped Amy off Villain. "I see you and Villain are getting very comfortable with each other."

"Are you jealous because you've tried to beat us on nearly every horse you own?" Amy linked her arm through his as they walked towards the picnic.

Ryan stopped and sighed when he saw they had company. "Looks like we have a third joining us today."

"Goldie." Amy unlinked her arm and ran to where the big red wolf lay on the picnic blanket as if he owned it. "He was looking after it for us."

"Sure, he was." Ryan eyed the wolf. He and Goldie were not quite besties, but they had a grudging respect for each because they both cared about Amy.

Amy watched Ryan sit down next to her opposite Goldie. She was so happy she thought she was going to burst. Amy had some news to tell Ryan, and she wasn't too sure how he would take it. But it was something Amy had to do, and even though they hadn't yet confessed how they felt about each other, Amy was sure Ryan felt the same about her as she did about him. She was confident that he'd understand why she had to do what needed to be done.

"Are we celebrating something?" Amy asked him, accepting a glass of wine from him.

Ryan surprised her by saying, "No, I just thought we could have our first official date. I know I didn't ask you like I should've, but I'm a bit rusty on the dating scene."

Amy's heart once again expanded as she stared at Ryan with his dark, brooding looks and gentle hazel eyes. She leaned forward and touched her lips to his.

"I love how you tricked me into our first date," Amy teased him.

Ryan loved her mischievous ways and how she managed to surprise him each day with some new hidden talent of hers. She was feisty and fierce when she needed to be, but so gently and kind. Amy was everything he'd never known he'd wanted in a relationship. He even loved how she loved to tease him. He smiled, and his arm snaked around her waist. He pulled her to him and started to kiss her senseless when his phone rang. Ryan ignored it at first and the thing went silent but started up ringing again not long after it had stopped. Ryan reluctantly released Amy, not letting her go too far from him. Sighing he pulled out his phone to answer it.

"Hello?" Ryan growled into the phone. It was West.

"Hi, is Amy with you?" West asked him. "She isn't answering her phone. I have to confirm our flights to LA for tomorrow, and she hasn't come back to me about her seat preference."

Ryan felt like someone had thrown a bucket of ice water over him as West's words seeped into his system and snaked through his veins like tiny arrows aiming at his heart. He stiffened and pulled away from Amy.

"Yes, she is here." Ryan's voice was clipped as he handed the phone to Amy.

He saw the confusion crease her brow as she reached out and took Ryan's phone.

"Hello?" Amy said into the phone.

Not wanting to hear more, Ryan stood up. He recorked the wine and dumped the contents of his wine glass. He took out the food and gave Goldie anything he knew was safe for the wolf – who had sensed his tension and stood up with him – could eat. Ryan packed up the picnic for his men to fetch later and walked over to gather the horses. To his surprise, Goldie followed him, and when he got to the horses, the big wolf nudged his head beneath Ryan's hand.

It was the first time Goldie had made any move for physical contact with him. As he gently and cautiously stroked the big wolf's head, he knew at that moment the animal understood what he was feeling.

"You knew she would leave eventually, didn't you, boy?" Ryan said softly to the wolf. "I guess she was never really ours. Someone as bright and talented as Amy deserves to shine her light on the world."

Goldie whined his agreement and licked Ryan's hand.

"All we can do is let her go," Ryan told the wolf, who looked up at him and gave him a soft bark.

Ryan wasn't sure if the animal was agreeing or disagreeing with him, but he didn't have time to find out when Amy ran up to him.

"Ryan, please wait. I can explain." Amy looked up at him pleadingly.

Ryan wanted to pull her to him and hold her until she agreed to stay, but he knew there were just some stars in the sky that you could never reach. They shone far too bright and too high. Amy was one of those stars. And after everything she'd been through, she deserved to take her place as one of the brightest stars again.

"It's okay, I understand." Ryan kept his voice level and his expression blank. "What we had was fun while it lasted, but we both knew this day was coming, Amy." He forced a smile onto his face. "I'm so happy for you, and you deserve to get back out there to show the world that nothing can keep the incredible Amy Guest down."

Ryan pulled her to him for what he hoped felt like a friendly hug and kissed her on the head.

"But we'd better get back so you can get ready to leave," Ryan told her. "I'm sure I heard West say he needed to fetch you by five this afternoon, and it is already three."

Ryan handed Amy Villain's reins and then helped her onto his back before swinging up onto Daisy's. He rode with her until the farmhouse was in sight and then made an excuse that he needed to go check out one of the boundary fences. Ryan said goodbye and wished her luck before turning Daisy around and riding off as fast as he could while he still had the strength to let her go.

❦

*A*my sat staring after Ryan and Daisy riding away from her. Her throat burned from her trying to swallow back the tears. As Ryan disappeared into the distance, she felt like her whole world had just tilted upside down. Amy was so sure Ryan had felt the same way about her and that he'd understand why she had to go back to LA. But as she stared at the now-empty horizon, hurt and confused, she knew she'd only been fooling herself.

Amy had got so caught up in all the romance of how he'd saved her more than once. With her crazy dreams of a spirit animal and her new wolf friend, she had convinced herself was it. Amy had been living in a fantasy world made up of what she'd always dreamed the perfect romance would be. She'd been so caught up in it all she'd even started to believe that Ryan was the hero of her story. Her soulmate.

But the cold reality was that Ryan had just been playing along with her. Probably amusing himself with the fact that he had the full attention and adoration of Amy Guest. Her pain turned to anger as the thought struck her. It had happened to her before, except that time Amy hadn't let herself fall as deep as she had for Ryan. But after everything Amy had been through, she would not let a bruised heart and ego break her.

No, she would hold her head high and do what she needed to do: face the world and clear both her and her brother's names. Earlier that morning, Wallace had told her that Martin didn't have anything to do with Amy being drugged. He'd been genuinely worried that his sister was going down the same slippery slope their father had. Martin's only crime was falling for that horrid Ursula and breaking Tammy's heart. Tammy, who had warned her to be careful with her heart around Ryan. Tammy, who had always been a sister to her.

Amy had too many people whose names needed to be cleared that had been tarnished by Ursula and Jason. Amy would carry her shattered heart in her hands if she had to hold all the pieces together until she had done what she needed to do. Once the world knew the truth from her, she would find a way to mend her heart and stop the bleeding in her soul. A shout from the ranch house caught her attention and made her turn to see Gwen calling her.

Amy wiped away the tears she hadn't even noticed were

running down her cheeks. She gathered all the strength she had left and plastered her plastic smile on her face as she galloped back to the house.

⚘

Their trip to Billings to catch a plane was delayed because Tammy was late getting back from the hike into the mountains. Zac, Cat, Chelsea, David, Tammy, Greg, Brett, Avery, Liam, and Wallace had set off before dawn. They were going to find out once and for all if Callum had hidden his and all the other five families' treasures and heirlooms in the mountain.

When they got back, it was amidst a sea of excitement. Cat's pendant had been the key to unlocking the stone door that hid more than just their family's treasures. It hid a cavern full of raw rubies that ran deep into the mountains. They hadn't brought back anything but a large old book that Cat took. It was and old family journal started by the first Sparrow to occupy the land. They now knew where all their family heirlooms, trunks from that attic, and David's grandfather's priceless collection had been hidden.

Cat called for all the ranches to meet the following day so she could tell them what she'd learned from the journal of the first Sparrow to have settled here. They made plans to meet early the following morning, and a wave of sadness washed over Amy as she thought she wasn't going to be there for it. In fact, Amy had decided to send for the rest of her things once she was in LA. She was not planning to come back. Even though she would miss the dear friends she'd made, Tammy, as well as her family, there was nothing else here for her.

All her friends had found a second chance at happiness while all she'd found was a fantasy that had turned into heartache. There was nothing for Amy to come back for. While West listened to the group's adventure, Amy snuck out the back and walked to the stables to say goodbye to Diamond, Fern, and

Villain. As she walked towards the stables, she looked around, hoping to see Goldie one last time to say goodbye. But the wolf was nowhere to be seen. She couldn't even feel his presence. It was like he had abandoned her too.

With a heavy heart, Amy walked into the stables. She made her rounds, stopping first at Fern's stable.

"You've got this, big girl." Amy stroked the horse's soft nose. "You'll see this time it will be different."

She kissed the horse's head before moving to say goodbye to Diamond and Villain. She was walking back into the other stalls when she stopped dead in her tracks as Ryan entered from the other side. He was leading Daisy into the stables. Her eyes caught a movement next to him, and she was shocked to see Goldie walking close to his side.

"Amy!" Ryan stopped too when he saw her standing there. "I thought you'd left by now."

"We were waiting for Tammy to return from her mountain hike," Amy told him, trying to keep her voice steady and her emotions under control. "There is a lot of excitement going on inside."

"I take it they found everything they were looking for then?" Ryan nodded.

"Yes, they did," Amy said awkwardly. It was getting harder to keep herself together. "I just came out to say goodbye to Diamond, Fern, and Villain."

"So, you really are going then?" Ryan's voice dropped.

"Yes." Amy nodded.

"I guess you won't be coming back?" Ryan's face was a mask of indifference as he stared at her.

"Is there really anything for me to come back for?" Amy asked him softly, hoping that he would ask her to stay.

They stood staring at each in silence for a few seconds before he spoke.

"I guess not." Ryan's voice was emotionless. "I'd better get Daisy brushed down."

Amy nodded. It was all she could do as she felt her heart

tumble when Ryan walked past her. She reached out toward Goldie, but he pulled away and moved closer to Ryan. When they were behind her, Amy closed her eyes as her heart hit the ground, shattering into a million shards. She knew she would never be able to piece it together ever again and had no reason to do it either. Her mother had been right; love was an emotion that caused nothing but pain, disillusion, and humiliation.

Still, all Amy wanted to do was crumble to the ground, pull herself into a ball, and cry until she ran out of tears. But West's call from the back door of the ranch pulled her back into the real world. Her world had forced her to once again step into character to play the part of Amy Guest; actress extraordinaire, fallen from grace, falsely accused of drug addiction while the evil Ursula Dougal and Jason Brown tried to steal her empire by using her brother. She straightened her shoulders, plastered on her plastic smile, and walked away from Montana. No one would even know that while she was telling the world her story, her heart lay in a million pieces on the stable floor of Four Lakes ranch.

"*I* can't believe the feud our families have supposedly been fueling all these years was over ownership of the ranches," Maria shook her head and sipped her glass of wine.

Cat, Maria, Chelsea, Tammy, and Amy had met at Big Valley Ranch, which belonged to Maria's family. They were having an evening glass of wine to have a pre-discussion of what was found in the mountain cavern. They had all ganged up on Cat and made her give them the CliffsNotes version of what was in the journal.

When the first Sparrow arrived in Lewistown there was nothing much here. He had arrived in the valley with his crewmen that were fleeing from the British Navy. Cat's ancestor had brought along his five closest friends who also turned out to be the crew members of his ship. They were privateers that were fleeing from the wrath of the British navy. The first Sparrow, Parker, Hitchin, Anderson, Beckett, and Donaldson had stuck together as they were not only crew members but the closest of friends.

When they'd first arrived in the valley, they had helped save one of the Native American tribe's villages and the chief's daughter. As a reward the chief had awarded Captain Sparrow a huge portion of land which he split six ways. But the land came with conditions and a sacred oath elicited from all six men. First the land could never be owned by anyone, but a Sparrow and the other five ranches could never be sold off. The land, although divided into different properties had to remain as one whole under the Sparrow family.

The large stone giants looked over and protected the valley below, holding treasures deep within them. Whoever owned the land below had to protect the treasures as well as the wild creatures that roamed around them. The treasures the mountains held deep within them turned out to be much sought-after rare rubies. One of which was given to Captain Sparrow to cement his sacred trust.

The six families lived side by side for a good few generations before the feud began. It got to a point where the Donaldsons packed up and left their land vacant until David's grandfather reclaimed it. In the mid-nineteen hundreds, the Donaldsons decided it was time to ignore a pact that had been made decades ago. They had occupied and worked their ranch for decades. They now wanted full ownership of it. But the Sparrows were adamant to fulfill the trust and oath that they had inherited through generations. It was their legacy and their sacred duty to the land.

This enraged the Donaldsons. They then incited the rest of the ranches to try and go up against the Sparrows and demand their land deeds become theirs. Unable to take it anymore the Sparrows had gotten their lawyers to draw up lease agreements.

This now stated that each ranch would have to lease their land and pay a levy to the Sparrows. It enraged the ranches even more and soon there were locked in a battle for the ownership of their land. All the Sparrows would say was none of them truly owned the land they all leased it from nature. What started out as what was supposed to be an amicable discussion between the Donaldsons and the Sparrows turned into a war of land between all six neighbors.

Through the years, though, the feud died down, but the families were still wary of each other. They only ever socialized at special occasions, funerals, weddings, and milestone birthdays. Other than that, they had remained angry at each other for not being able to own their land due to some ancient pact Captain Sparrow had made. At the end of telling her friends what she had found Cat felt relieved. Now they understood what the feud was about they could do something about it. The friends saluted to the end of the feud and the end of the reign of terror the Brown's had brought down on them for years.

"Now that is out of they way," Tammy said. "How are we going to get Ryan and Amy back together."

"I was hoping Gwen would be here tonight," Maria told them. "We need her help with Ryan." She frowned at Cat. "Do you know where Gwen is?"

"She's out on a date with Jude," Tammy said with a huge smile on her face. "We are all so happy for them both. No two people deserve to be happy like they do."

"I agree," Cat said, holding up her glass in a salute. "But I don't think we should go meddling in Amy and Ryan's personal business."

"Of course, we're going to meddle," Chelsea told Cat. "As Amy and Ryan's friends it's our job to meddle."

"Especially if it means making sure they both find happiness," Tammy backed up Chelsea. "And I want both Ryan and Amy to be as happy as we all are now that we're with our second chances at romance."

"I agree with Tammy," Chelsea said, sipping her wine. "It's meddling time."

"I have a plan for that," Maria grinned, leaning in to let her friends in on her suggestion about how to get Amy and Ryan back together.

"For the record," West said as he watched three cars pull up in the Billings mall parking lot where Tammy had insisted, he was to meet them at five in the morning, "I think this is a terrible idea."

"Oh, hush!" Molly shushed him. "This is a brilliant idea, and as Gwen said, no two people were ever meant to be together as those two are."

"And just how do you lot," West glanced over and raised his eyebrows in disbelief when he saw Greg, Zac, Brett, David, and Wallace walk towards him, "Intend to get Ryan to Billings?"

"We've left that up to my daughter," Gwen said with a big smile. "Trust me, if anyone can get Ryan here, that's Avery."

"I shudder to think of how she's going to do that." West shook his head and reluctantly took out his phone. "Amy and I better not miss our flights."

"Did you get the other ticket?" Maria walked over to him and kissed his cheek.

"Of course, I did." West sighed. He scrolled through his phone and dialed Amy's number.

It rang a few times before she answered it.

"West? Where are you?" She hissed through the receiver.

"I've been delayed by a business meeting I had to take," West lied. "I'll be there in twenty minutes. Don't worry, I've already checked us in, and the airline wouldn't dare leave without Amy Guest."

"You'd better hope so!" Amy said angrily. "I'll be waiting in the coffee shop." She hung up.

"There. Are you all happy?" West looked at them.

"Not yet," Molly answered for them all. "Now come on, we'd better get moving. Avery just let Cat know that she and Ryan are nearly at the airport. You don't want to miss your flight," she tutted, making West roll his eyes.

"I don't see why I couldn't just go to the airport with Amy," West muttered as he followed Maria to her car.

"Because then Amy wouldn't have to go hide in a coffee shop so she wouldn't be recognized." Maria laughed at the look West gave her.

⌒

"Avery, I can't believe you got me up at midnight to drive you to the Billings airport," Ryan hissed as they pulled into the parking. He didn't want to be anywhere near this airport, especially on this particular day.

"I told you that I have something very important to deliver to Amy," Avery told him through gritted teeth.

"But why did I have to bring you?" Ryan muttered as his niece grabbed his hand and nearly dragged him into the airport building.

"Oh, stop complaining!" Avery frowned at him as she pulled her towards a coffee shop. "I tell you what, why don't you go in there and grab us a coffee while I go find Amy."

"Fine!" Ryan needed a cup anyway.

"Oh, and can you keep this for me?" Avery slipped something into his pocket. "I don't want to lose it."

Before he could answer her, she was gone. Ryan stood staring after her, confused and wondering what the heck was up with his niece today. He shook his head. Ryan hadn't been asleep when Avery had come to ask him to drive her here. He was tossing and turning. Thoughts of Amy were swirling through his head and tormenting him even when he didn't have his eyes closed. To top it off, when had managed to doze, it was to dream about his wolf, and her message kept echoing through his head.

*Sometimes, setting someone free isn't always the answer because sometimes those you are trying to set free have actually come back home to you.*

Ryan shook the thoughts off and walked toward a table when he bumped into someone walking to the same table. He stopped and was about to apologize when his breath caught in his throat.

"Amy!" Ryan's voice sounded raspy, as if the word had been scrapped out from his heart.

"Ryan!" Amy's eyes widened in shock, and her face paled. "What are you doing here?"

"I had to..." He trailed off. Something told him to feel in his pocket. He slipped his hand in and felt the small item in there. He closed his eyes and swallowed as the wolf's words echoed through his head once again. "I was looking for you." He opened his eyes and looked into hers.

"I..." Amy took a step back and looked up at him. "I don't understand."

"Amy, I never should've let you go!" Ryan knew he couldn't keep what he felt for her in anymore. She wasn't a star that was out of his reach. She was his soul mate, his heart, his home.

"Ryan..." Amy's eyes misted over as she looked at him, confused.

"Yesterday, you asked if there was anything for you to come back to Four Lakes for." Ryan cleared his throat. "You have no idea how hard it was for me not to grab you and tell you there was everything for you to come back for."

"Like what?" Amy stared up at him, and he could see her fight to control her emotions like he had yesterday.

"Me!" Ryan said softly. "Yesterday, the picnic was supposed to be special because I wanted to finally confess to you just how deeply in love with you."

Amy bit her lip, and a tear spilled onto her cheek. Ryan leaned forward and wiped it away with his thumb while his hand cupped her soft cheek.

"You hurt me," Amy's voice wobbled as she sucked in a shaky breath.

"I didn't mean to," Ryan's voice dropped. "That last thing on this earth I ever wanted to do was hurt you. I thought that if I stepped aside, you'd be free to get back out into the world and do what you loved. What you were so clearly born to do — shine!" He cleared his throat again. "I didn't want to hold you back."

"How could you think I was supposed to shine when you are the light inside me?" Amy stopped fighting and let the tears fall as her hand covered his on her cheek.

"Because he's a complete idiot!" Avery's voice made them look around.

Their eyes widened as they saw a sea of familiar faces standing and watching them.

"Great!" Ryan laughed and dropped his forehead onto Amy's. "I'm sorry about our audience."

"That's fine. At least they are an audience of people who love us," Amy sniffed. "What made you change your mind?"

"My crazy niece," Ryan said softly. "Where do we go from here?"

"I have to go to LA, Ryan," Amy told him, looking into his eyes. "I wanted to ask you if you would come with me yesterday." She swallowed. "Because I couldn't bear to spend one day without you."

"I would love to, but I don't have anything with me," Ryan said.

"Well..." Avery stepped forward and showed him the back-pack she'd brought with her. "You kinda do."

"Of course, I do." Ryan laughed and then remembered what Avery had shoved into his pocket. "Yesterday at the picnic, there was something I needed to ask you but never got around to it. I wanted to ask you when we were on our own and in a better setting." He glanced at the expectant faces of his family and friends. "But I guess it's more about the timing than the setting that makes certain moments special."

"Okay?" Amy frowned, looking confused.

Her eyes widened as she saw Ryan drop down onto one knee and pull a beautiful blue velvet box from his pocket, which opened to show a beautiful diamond ring.

"Amy Guest, will you marry me?" Ryan held the ring up to her. "I don't want to spend another day without you either. I love you."

Amy stared down at him incredulously before her hand closed around his, and she smiled as the tears slid down her cheeks. "Yes!" was all she said.

Ryan sprang to his feet, fumbled with the ring as he put it on her finger, and then pulled her to him to seal their engagement with a kiss.

The people in the coffee shop had all stopped to watch the scene unfold and broke into a chorus of applause.

"And you thought this was a bad idea!" Molly looked smugly at West.

"I guess it was just meant to be." West grinned.

⚭

As the sun rose over the valley that housed Cupids Bow Ranch, Mountain Rise Ranch, Big Valley Ranch, Donaldsons Ranch, and Four Lakes Ranch, it brought with it a new era – one that promised peace and prosperity as love blossomed in each of the houses. The balance was once again restored. The large stone giant that stood tall looking out for the valley below was once against safe and its treasures protected.

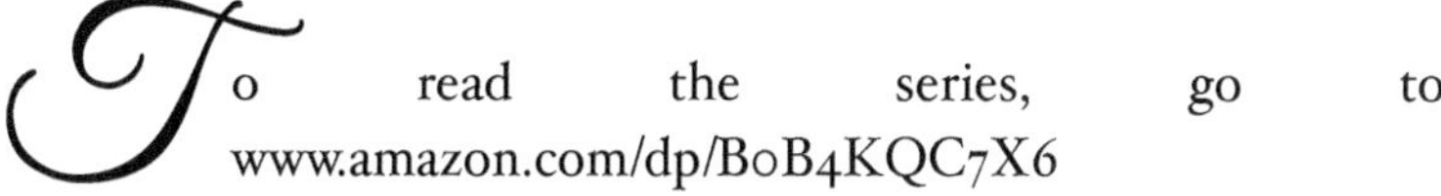

## THE NEXT ADVENTURE

ARE YOU READY TO READ Manatee Bay: Beginnings, prequel to the Treasure Seeker Beach Series?

To read the series, go to www.amazon.com/dp/B0B4KQC7X6

# ALSO BY AMY RAFFERTY

To dive into your next read, go to https://www.amyraffertyauthor.com/

## STAY UPDATED WITH ME

Thank you so much for purchasing or downloading my book! I am grateful to all my amazing readers.

To stay updated on all my latest books, newsletters, freebies and beautiful photos from the fabulous locations I write about, why not join my VIP group?

I will send you regular pictures of La Jolla Cove, San Diego and the Florida Gulf Beaches where I try to spend as much time as I can. I live in San Diego, my own 'Garden Of Eden' and I am in love with the sea and the beaches in the area. They inspire me to write lots of beachy mystery romance fiction to share with my awesome readers like you. To join me go to https://landing.mailer lite.com/webforms/landing/y6w2d2

You will be asked for your email. You also get a FREE BOOK whenever you sign-up!

Amazon #1 Best-Seller, Amy Rafferty is a contemporary romance author of feel-good beach romance reads with heartwarming stories embracing humor and love.

Born in New York, previously a Lawyer, she now lives in San Diego with her beautiful children and cats!

Aside from writing, publishing and running her home, she spends as much time as she can visiting the beautiful San Diego and Florida beaches where she has family and friends. She calls San Diego her 'Garden of Eden', inspiring her to write clean and wholesome romance novels incorporating mystery, suspense and adventures for her characters as they find a way to open their hearts and let true love in.

facebook.com/amyraffertyauthor

instagram.com/amyraffertyauthor